D1529002

Can You Keep a Secret?

Omegia Keeys

Passionate Writer Publishing

Indiana

Passionate Writer Publishing

www.passionatewriterpublishing.com

©2010 Omegia Keeys

ISBN 13 978-0-9843504-7-6

ISBN 10 0-9843504-7-0

Manufactured in the United States of America.

First Edition

Omegia Keeys

Also by

Omegia keeys

Passionate Playmates

(2006, 2010)

Seduction.com

(2009)

"Seduction.com" by Omegia Keeys is an exciting and fascinating novel that I recommend to everyone. It's a must read involving men, money, and sex!

4.0 out of 5 stars **Men, Money and Sex**, March 7, 2010 Tekisha OOSA Online Book Club "O.O.S.A. Gets It Read!"

Keeys did a fantastic job at keeping the readers interest with an amazing plot and smooth transitions. I loved Seduction.com giving it ***** **(5) Stars**, BK Walker, reviewer for BK Walker Books

Dedications

This is dedication to all the women out there in search of finding themselves, or just a fresh start. Just remember while you are finding yourself be careful that you don't get lost.

Chapter 1

I sat at the top of the stairs, waiting for him to come home. I came home to surprise him, but the surprise was on me. The pink thongs peeking out from underneath our bed stood out like a sore thumb. I hadn't been home in two weeks, so there was no way those were mine. I sat my purse down on the dresser, and that's when I noticed it. A bottle of perfume, mixed in with my Victoria Secret body spray.

This mutha has lost his freaking mind! No, he didn't have some woman in MY home, OUR home!

I picked up the bottle of perfume, a knock off brand, and threw it at the wall, shattering a picture of him and me.

This bastard screwed this woman with our picture looking down on them!

I should have known something was wrong. The boys were not outside playing when I pulled up. We had twins, age 9. The boys had summer camp until 3:30, and should have been home for an hour before he made it home. Our retired next-door neighbors always kept an eye out for the boys until either I or Jamal (the mutha in question) made it home. I whipped out my cell, calling the camp just to find out that the boys had not been there in a week. I thought that was strange, so I called Angela, my younger sister.

"Have you seen the boys?"

"Yeah, I have them. Jamal said he wanted to come and surprise you for a week, so I kept them for him. What's going on?"

"Oh really? Look, I will fill you in later," I said, abruptly hanging up the phone.

For a week? He had some whore in my house for a week?

I heard the keys jiggling in the door and then in he came. Jamal was so busy on the phone, he didn't even notice me sitting at the top of the stairs. The dang alarm system was beeping so loud that it drowned out the conversation he was having. I had set the alarm back once I was inside. It was my attempt to maintain my surprise. By the time Jamal disabled it, he was off the phone.

Can You Keep a Secret?

Get your ass up these stairs. I heard cabinets open and close, then ice coming from the refrigerator dispenser. Finally, footsteps back in the direction of the stairs.

"Hey baby," Jamal, said when he finally noticed me. It sounded like he was more aggravated than happy to see me. "What are you doing back so early? I thought you had two more days at your conference."

He tried to give me a kiss, but I moved to the side. I did not know where or on who those lips had been.

"Hi," I said dryly. I wanted to slap the mess out of Jamal. Instead, I held up the thong by the waistband with two fingers. I was not taking any chances of getting coochie juice getting on me. "Whose are these?"

"How should I know? Where did you get them?"

Are you serious? You are NOT trying to act like I just picked up some random chicks funky draws and brought them with me.

"I found them by the bed. Who did you have in my home, Jamal?" It really did not matter what he said. I knew it was going to be a lie.

"Man, I thought I told you my mom was coming in town. She changed up in here and must have dropped them," he lied.

Sucka we live in a 4 bedroom, two story home, with a full basement and only two kids. And, they obviously have

3

not been here in the past week. Despite all that, you expect me to believe she changed up in our room. Not to mention she was 60 years old, eww.

"So what about the perfume on the dresser?"

Cheap ass heifa!

"It must be hers too."

I wanted to kick his tail and tear up the house with his lying ass. Instead, I resorted to being me--the peaceful, loving wife.

"Okay, where are the boys?" This time I let him kiss me on the cheek.

Jamal pulled me up off the stairs and gave me a big hug.

"They are at your sister's. The camp was closed this week. I still had to work. I was actually going to come and surprise you, but I picked up a big client at the last minute. But lucky me, you are home early."

Yeah, luck you. Lucky I didn't come home and catch you with that other woman and took both of ya'll out.

It was already late and I was worn out from my flight. I told Jamal I needed to lie down and get some rest. He took the hint and did not try to have sex with me, not that it would have done much for me anyway.

When we first met in college everything was like a fairy tale. He was a halfback on the football team, and had a full ride scholarship. The players had mandatory study tables at the same time as the track team (which I was on). I didn't have a full ride--more like 75%, but the good grades I had brought in some grants to cover the rest.

At first, I thought he was a dummy like most of the other male athletes. Then, he had me oversee one of his business plans for class. Let me tell you, he was not only smart, but it was the layout for his company that he owns today. So, you can say I fell for his mind. It didn't hurt that he was sexy as well. He was six feet two inches, a body that had never missed a day in the gym; still to this day, brown skinned, kept a low fade, and well trimmed goatee. Hell, Jamal was one of the sexiest men on campus. Even the fraternity brand on his right bicep was sexy.

During college, the sex was the bomb, or at least that's what I thought. He would come over, bang my back out, get his release, and leave me in a pool of sweat. I had never had an orgasm so I did not know the difference either way. It was good to me.

Fast forward ten years later. When we have sex, I wait for him to start snoring so I can finish myself off. I had stayed up late one night a few years prior, while he was out of town, and caught this sex talk show. The lady was old as dirt, but she kept me interested. Now if this old crow knew how to find the g-spot, then what the heck was wrong with me? I did everything she said, and oh my freaking goodness, I came! It was the most glorious thing in the world. I never knew that was how it was supposed to be. So yeah baby, go to sleep so I can get mine.

Chapter 2

Who the heck is calling me this early? And, where in the heck is Jamal? I know I wasn't that dang tired.

"Hello?"

"Mo, you up girl?"

"Angela? What time is it?" I answered fumbling around to find my glasses. I have the faintest clue why, but it seems like I cannot hear right unless my glasses are on. Helps me focus I guess.

"Never mind the time. What the heck went on last night? You called and asked if I had the kids. Then it dawned on me. You must be in town. Because, if Jamal would have went to see you, then you would have already

7

known that. So like I said, what the heck is going on?"
Angela asked, a little too perky for 8:00am, on my day off.

"If you must know, nosey, I came back to surprise
Jamal." I was not ready to go into detail about the rest of it.

"And? Cause I know there was something crazy
behind this. He didn't dump these boys on me for no
reason. I mean I love my nephews, but they need to sit
down sometime. They are eating me out of house and
home," she paused, waiting for an answer. "Mo?"

"Huh, oh yeah. I found some thongs on the floor." I
got side tracked walking around the house trying to find
Jamal.

"Some thongs? As in some lady's thongs? Is Jamal
still alive? I know you let him have it," she said loudly in
my ear.

"I mean, he said they were his mom's. She came in
town for the weekend…" I started saying.

Cutting me off, Angela said, "I don't look like
Boo Boo the Fool, and I know you don't. His mom? Don't
make me slap you through this phone! I know you don't
believe that mess?"

"No, not really." I had to admit.

"Not really? Girl, call me back when you have
found my sister. What has happened to you? When we

were younger, you never fell for crap like this. I can't take this. I am gone."

No she didn't! This heifa hung up on me. Got the nerve to call me early as heck and then hang up on me. What happened to me is, I got married and had two boys. I have an obligation...hold on? Doesn't he have an obligation to the boys and me as well?

I searched the whole house and did not see Jamal anywhere. He normally didn't leave the house until 8:30am.

He must have read my mind, because my cell was ringing, playing his ring tone.

"Hey baby. You awake yet?"

"I am now." *And I ain't your baby.*

I been thinking and I know I should have told you about my mom coming up to stay with us. That underwear thing looks rather crazy. How about I take you out tonight and make it up to you.

How about you eating rat poison so you can quit feeding me this bull.

"Sure baby. When should I be ready?"

"I won't be off until about six but I have a change of clothes here. I'll be ready when I come get you."

I once thought it was a nice idea to have his office with the shower built in it. Now I'm not so sure he was only using it after coming from the gym.

Great, now you have several hours to bang some whore, while I do what? Unpack?

"That's fine. I may go by Angela's, see the boys, and let her know we will be going out, so she can keep them a little longer."

"Ok, it's a date." He said it just like when he used to really take me out on dates. Not the ones to McDonald's like in college, but the real ones like the dates right before we got married.

I hung up the phone and went to take a shower. I twisted the dial head to massage and let the water beat my muscles. I was stiff and sore from sleeping uncomfortably. I didn't want Jamal anywhere near me, so I stayed on my side of the bed, in the same position, all night long. The water beating my skin relaxed me, melting away the tension. I was lucky. He finally listened and had the water softener installed. A few months back when I tried to take a shower like this and the water almost tore my skin off. It was so hard that I had to cover up my nipples, to protect them from the punches that the faucet spit out.

Stepping out the shower, I caught my reflection in the mirror. There I was all 5ft 6 inches of me. I weighed barely 130 pounds and that was because of muscle mass. I was nowhere near a body builder, but I would give Angela Bassett a run for her money. You know, when she played Tina Turner and she had those cut up arms? I worked my abs back into a flat tummy after having those boys of mine. It was hard work, but I did it. In the beginning, I was reminded of the c-section with each crunch, or sit-up I did. My stomach felt like it was going to literally rip in half. Now, the only reminder is my 5-inch bikini cut incision and a few stretch marks that could only be seen at certain angles. I had caramel color skin (more like bronze now that it was summer) and I was very pretty. I wouldn't say sexy. When I think of sexy, I think of those video girls with all the make-up. That wasn't me at all.

I got my hair cut a few months back, and I am loving it. No more long and flowing for me. Bye-bye two hours under the dryer. Hello in and out the beauty shop in an hour and a half. The transformation was amazing. I looked like I was still in high school with all that hair, especially when it was time to get it done again. I would whip it up in a ponytail with the quickness and call it a day. Now my hair was low in the back and the rest curled. I kept my long bangs though. Most days, I swooped them behind my ear, with my glasses holding them in place. Now, I look like I actually had those twin boys of mine.

It was almost 90 degree's out yesterday, so I was expecting more of the same today. I dug through my closet in search of a nice summer dress to wear. I needed something that would still be nice this evening, just in case my sister gets to running her mouth and I don't make it back in time to change. I ended up choosing my white, gold, and blue dress with a high waist belt, more of a classy and sophisticated look. It matched perfectly to these gold wedge heeled sandals I picked up down in Georgia.

"Took you long enough," Angela said when I got to her house.

"Like you knew I was coming," I replied. I did not bother to call first.

"I thought you would have been on your way after our conversation this morning. So did you find the real you?"

"Stop. You act like this is easy."

"I know it's not, but you need to put him out, now." I know she wanted to say more but my little men came running into the living room.

"Hey mommy!" they sang in unison, giving me the reception I deserved.

"Hey Double J!" Now these two are my hearts. I called them "Double J" when they were together, because their names were Jaylen and Jayden. The boys were fraternal twins but they still looked almost identical. You have to have them standing side by side not moving around, to see the slight difference. Jaylen was an inch taller, and each boy had a mole, but the on opposite chin. Jayden was also left handed, but you wouldn't know that unless he was eating or writing.

"You back early? Did daddy come back early too?" Jaylen asked. He was the inquisitive one. Jayden could care less. As long as it did not affect him, Jayden remained silent.

"Yeah, he's here too," I answered. I had to ignore Angela rolling her eyes behind my baby head.

"Can we stay the night again?" Jayden spoke up. Angela looked as if she was a bobble head with all the 'hell no's' she was mouthing. "We really went want to spend the night next door. Chris's mom asked if we could." Angela started smiling then.

"Well that is fine with me. I mean , as long as your auntie is okay with it. I know how she loves spending time with you," I said with a straight face.

And just as fast as they ran in the room, they were gone again. That was how the twins were though. They were happy just to know I was in the vicinity.

"Whatever! You wrong for that. I will think twice before I say yes to a week ever again," she said.

"What the heck are you watching on TV?" I asked, trying to give her something else to focus on instead of my issues.

"The First 48. I love this show. It goes over how they try to catch murderers within the first 48 hours. They say if it goes past that time frame, there is a less chance in solving the crime."

Angela was all into forensic science. She watched all the CSI shows too, Miami, New York, Las Vegas, even NCIS. She had her Bachelor's in Criminology and was focusing on Forensic Science for her Master's. I call her a career student, because it seems like she has been in school forever. She did two years of college and got pregnant her sophomore year, so she sat out a year. Then she went back, taking a couple classes here and there. Thank goodness for online classes, because now she can speed up her Master's with those accelerated programs.

A commercial came on, and she jumped right back on my case.

"So, when you gonna put him out?"

"Look, we are going to dinner tonight. We are going to talk over a few things."

"You mean he is going to lie, and you are going to be the good wife and play nice."

Can You Keep a Secret?

I won't be so good if I knocked you out your chair, now will I?

"Give me a break. I just got home. I am not that gullible. You are starting to actually hurt my feelings, you know," I said. I was trying to hold back the tears but they came rushing over the lids of my eyes faster than Katrina took out New Orleans.

"Dang. I'm sorry, sis. I wasn't trying to hurt you. You're right. You have been through enough. I will leave it alone," she said, hugging me. I knew that only meant she would leave me alone for now.

Chapter 3

I hear Jamal's mouth moving, but for some reason, I can't make out what he is saying. It sounded something like he wanted us to have a fresh start and come clean on a few things.

He picked me up from the house a little after six, like he said. I actually did have time to come home and change. Angela had to study for a test, but I chose not to. Jamal opened up the car door and everything for me. He even held his arm out for me to take. He brought me to the Eagle's Nest. He knew it was my favorite restaurant, because I can look down on Indianapolis while I ate. Our meal was delicious. Now we were waiting on desert.

"Look, baby I know I was wrong and I can admit that. Now, if you had of listened to me about going to all these different conferences, then this would not have happened," Jamal was saying.

"Like I had a choice, I am the Human Resources Manager for People's Insurance. How could I not go to our Conferences? Yes, it has been three, but that's where our other branches are Atlanta, Dallas, and Chicago. Come on now, you really can't count Chicago, it's three hours away. I also asked you to meet me up there."

"Well, I own my business so you know I could not go. I make enough for the both of us. I told you years ago that you can quit at any time."

"And any time has not happened for me yet. I love my job. Plus, I had at least a week in between each conference, during which, I came home." There was no way in the world I was going to quit my job. My degree was in HR, so what was I supposed to do let it collect dust? How could I encourage my kids to go out and do something for themselves if I didn't even follow my own dreams?

"See that's what I was saying, if you had not of gone, none of this would have happened." There he goes again with that if I had not left, this would not have happened stuff.

"Jamal, what are you saying?"

"I cheated. There I said it. If you were home, this wouldn't have happened," he said, tossing his dinner napkin on the table.

No shit. I know you cheated. I wasn't buying the BS you were selling. Hold on, did he say this was my fault?

"If I would have stayed home you would not have cheated?" I asked slowly trying to comprehend the madness.

"A man needs his woman by his side. I can't guarantee what will happen when I get lonely, with you running around the country."

Where the hell is this waiter with our check?

"Are you kidding me? We have a black man in the White House with a powerful black woman, who can hold her own, and you want me to quit my job and do what? Stay at home and twiddle my thumbs? Our kids are not babies!"

"You could pick up a hobby or something." I think he almost laughed at that himself.

"A hobby? I know what this is about. It's about how much I make. You have been on this kick ever sense I was promoted to upper management. I wanted to start my own temp agency, but you convinced me that it would be hard enough with you owning your own company. So what did I do, I backed down. But two years ago, that position came open. I took it. You dang right I took it. It should have been mine after the first 3 years with them. I was doing the job already any way."

"You want too much. You are almost like a man. I need someone who has my back."

"I have your back. I always have. This is the one thing I have ever wanted for myself," I whined.

"Well, if you continue to travel. I don't know what to tell you."

"I do." I said. "You can get your stuff and get out of my home. I do not have to deal with this. If I go out of town, you will cheat. You know I have to go again."

I can't believe I said that, but yes, get your shit! You better call Tyrone, or somebody but you got to go!

"See, this is exactly what I am talking about. You are acting like a man." He said as his face turned red.

I was so happy to see that waiter come with the check. Jamal was fuming. He was so mad that he could not even find the words to say anything back to me. He was so used to me standing my ground and then slowly backing off. Not this time. I didn't do anything wrong, and I was not going to be punished for it with a cheating husband. Who knows how long this mess has been going on. He better pray I don't have any diseases. I was not showing

Omegia Keeys

any symptoms, but that was not going to stop me from going to get checked out.

We sat in silence the entire way home. I know he probably wanted to put me out but he was driving my Benz and not his Escalade. It was one thing to have to sit in silence to the madness at work. All these people in an uproar about the Healthcare Reform Bill. They claim we are going to be put out of business. No, what we need to be put out of business for are these expensive policies we have. People pay an arm and a leg for our insurance. We don't cover more than half of what they need it for. If it is covered, most of them are only getting 80% paid. Our company would find loopholes in order to drop coverage on cancer patients. Claiming lame pre-existing conditions such as none disclosure of teenage acne. Some life saving procedures have been deemed experimental and denied, when doctors have been practicing them for years. We were flat out ripping people off and leaving some of them to die on a daily basis.

Jamal and I pulled into the garage. He got out, slamming his door and left me sitting there as if I did not know the way. I waited a few moments before walking in behind him. He was already upstairs lying across the bed.

No my brotha you got to go! Get to packing...chop, chop.

"I am serious, Jamal. I want you out tonight." He gave me the look of death, grabbed a few items, and left.

I, on the other hand, slumped into a ball of fear on the floor. I was scared of being alone, scared that he may come back, and scared because I've never stood my ground. Never stood on my own two feet.

Chapter 4

I hated going to family gatherings, for one reason in particular: my sister-in-law. Andrea, spotted me the moment I walked in my parent's house.

"Monica, where's Jamal? You know you can't go nowhere without him joined to your hip." I could smell the alcohol on her breath.

Like you don't already know that I put his cheating ass out over two weeks ago. He has made zero effort to try and come back home. Not that I would have let him, but dang.

"He couldn't make it this weekend. You know, he does work on the weekend," I responded with a lie.

"More like workout," Andrea snickered.

Can You Keep a Secret?

"And what is that supposed to mean?"

"You know a man can't be with one woman. You will take him back. I know you. You can't be without a man. You have always been spoiled. Welcome to the real world," she said, slurring her words. Having done her damage, Andrea turned in search of someone else to harass.

I wanted to slap the smirk off Andrea's face. I have dealt with that woman's abuse for over 15 years. Andrea had been jealous of me from the moment she laid eyes on me. For some reason, she felt that I had everything handed to me on a silver platter. Nothing I did or said could ever change that. The fact that I made good grades, earning scholarships and grants to college, had a job since I was 16, bought my own clothes in high school, and that my father hated me for being a girl when I was younger, didn't mean anything. In Andrea's eyes, I just sat back and things fell in my lap. When I was in high school, Andrea called me the spoiled track star. Yeah, I was on the team, but was always in the background until my junior year. One of the true stars got hurt and coach pulled me from my alternate position on the relay, to the 4th leg. It just so happens that on that day we were running the Penn Relays. I got that stick when we were loosing to four other teams. The next thing I know my body took over, walking the other girls down, winning the relay.

When I got to college, it was spoiled college girl. Like my parents where paying for it or something. The only thing I got from my mother was $20 here and there for gas money to come home. My father could have cared less. When I came home, Andrea would make smart remarks like, "not everyone can afford to go to college like Monica."

The funny thing is, Andrea's family had money. If she wanted to go to college, she could have. Andrea's mother always kept her in the latest designer clothes and hairdos. Andrea never knew what it was like to go with out electricity, heat, or water. I used to lie to my friends in school when our phone was disconnected, saying I was grounded and could not talk. Cable was a luxury only lasting until the first bill came, or until the cable company came and cut the line from us stealing it.

Our actual lives and the one Andrea perceived were the complete opposite. Andrea was the spoiled one, while I was the one who had to work for everything I was given.

"Hey baby, sis." My brother Jason (and Andrea's husband) came up behind me, giving me a kiss on the cheek. I have always wondered how my brother could be so sweet and end up with someone like Andrea. He gave her the world. She stomped all over him every chance she got.

But, Jason never complained, at least not to any family member.

"Jason," I said, giving him the biggest hug I could. I could feel Andrea's eyes boring a hole into the back of my shirt. It wouldn't be long before she came back over spreading her hate around. She could not stand the relationship that I had with my brother. "I missed you. How have you been?"

"I should be asking you that. You okay little sis?" He always had to rub that 'little' part in, all because he came out two minutes before me.

"I am good," I said. Surprisingly, I was actually telling the truth. I was handling the situation a lot better than I thought I would. I think somewhere along the line I still loved Jamal, but fell out of love with him. I had slowly been discovering the new me, doing the things that I wanted to do.

"Well you sure looked good," he said.

Jason always said things like that to me. He always said I should have been a model or something. There was no way I was getting out there for people to tell me all the things wrong with me. He was my brother. He was supposed to say things like that.

"So, where is your real twin?" Andrea asked, walking her funky attitude back over to us. She was referring to Angela. We did favor each other. She had a few more pounds than me, but Andrea knew how to work those hips and have the men fighting to get to her in a club.

"Why you wanna know?" Angela asked, walking up behind Andrea, and catching her off guard.

"I just haven't seen you, is all," Andrea lied. She knew not to mess with Angela. Angela has flung that woman around a time or two in the past.

"Well, now you see me. Go find you some business while us siblings catch up." Angela said, dismissing her. Andrea took off in the direction of the kitchen.

"No that heifa didn't think she can come up in my Momma house disrespecting folks. I know she is your wife, Jason, but why so serious?" She said it just like the Joker in the *Dark Knight* movie. Jason and I fell out laughing. He knew his wife was crazy and didn't try to hide it.

"We all need to quit. We are supposed to be celebrating Mom and Dad's 35th anniversary, right?" Jason said, getting us off the subject of his wife before Angela really got started.

Thirty-five years is a long time. It's even longer when one part of the couple had checked out on the marriage a long time ago. Our dad was a doting husband the first five years and non-existent for almost 25. Then, a few years ago, he came around and quit running the streets.

I wondered how our mom stuck in the marriage so long. She always said he would come around one day, bet she didn't know it would be over 20 plus years later.

We walked out to the backyard where everything was set up. My parent's old friends were standing up, making speeches and jokes about them. I glanced over at the couple and they truly did look happy. My dad no longer had the scowl on his face that I had grown accustomed to. When their friends were quiet, the hired DJ (our cousin Levi) put on their favorite song, *At Last*, by Etta James. Or, maybe he was playing Beyonce's version. Heck, they both sounded good to me.

My father took my mother's hand in his and pulled her into him. He whispered something in her ear. She giggled, then they started dancing. The moment was so beautiful. Everyone was taking pictures. The photographer had a hard time getting a good shot, because everyone else was blocking his view. He resorted to standing on a chair. He must have known my mom. She would have torn that photographer a new one if they did not get their monies worth.

I stayed in the back yard for almost an hour just taking in my family. My crazy uncle was doing the same old tired dance the man had done since I was a little girl. He was still wearing his dress socks pulled up to his knees as well. What the heck was up with that? My mom's best friend, Ann, was trying to find her a sweet young thang to dance with. She did not care if the men were married, with someone, or claiming to be gay. Aunt Ann was determined. I was sipping on my drink, having a good laugh at her when I felt my phone vibrate. It was Yahoo sending me a text, letting me know I had an email. I went to my Yahoo account through my phone and read it. It was a message back from *Fantasy Girls*. The owner wanted to meet with me.

I was trying not to smile too hard, to avoid my family asking questions. In the search for me to find myself, I wanted to start with getting to know my body better and tapping into my sexuality. Seeing that old lady on TV expressing her sexuality so freely, those years back, had stirred something in me. I wanted to explore it more.

Chapter 5

"I looked over your resume and it says you are a Human Resources Manager?" Ecstasy asked. She told me she had reviewed several applications and had not been impressed over the last few weeks. That is, until she ran across one in particular. This one she decided to give a closer look. I assumed she was referring to me.

"You know you didn't have to submit a resume. A little background history and why you were interested in becoming a *Fantasy Girl* would have been just fine," Ecstasy continued.

"I understand. Is it going to be a problem? I just, well, I have no experience in this type of thing at all. As matter of fact, this is so not like me at all. The truth is, I am getting a divorce from my husband, and I want a fresh start. He would have never agreed to anything like this," I replied quietly. I sat up straight in the chair, poised like I had been trained in charm school. This whole interview was making me nervous.

Ecstasy sat there, eyeing me so hard that I could almost read her thoughts. Something like: *Her short haircut was simple, but cute. It was perfect for the corporate world. She wore makeup, not too much, just a little to enhance her beauty. The outfit she had on was something I would have passed up in Nostrums.* I willed her to say something, anything.

"Well, have you ever talked dirty to a man?"

"You mean, like phone sex?" I blushed.

"That's close to what it's like. I mean, have you ever told a man what you wanted him to do to you, or what you wanted to do to him?"

"A little," I said, smiling.

"Come on now. You have never told someone you were with that you couldn't wait for them to stick their penis inside you?" Ecstasy whispered to me, mindful of the other Starbuck's patrons.

"No. I wanted to, but I always let my ex-husband take charge," I replied honestly.

"Well honey, at *Fantasy Girls* you will have plenty of opportunity. I tell you what. I will look seriously into giving you a chance. In the meantime, you need to brush up on your skills. Read some books about turning your man on and seducing him. This book I read by Zane has some good examples. Heck, even try those articles in Cosmo. As a matter of fact, go to a strip club and get a lap dance."

"A lap dance? I am not gay?" I wasn't too sure about letting some other woman rub all up on me.

"Girl please, you do not have to be gay or bisexual to get a lap dance. It will help you learn your own body. Believe me, I had to come out of my shell too when I first got in this line of business," Ecstasy reassured me.

"If you say so." I replied. I wasn't, but I wanted this job and was willing to try anything.

"I will call you in a few days, okay? I expect you to tell me what you learned." Ecstasy got up from the table and left me sitting there in awe. She was beautiful and so sure of herself, without being cocky. She told me her real name was Erika, but I just loved the sound of Ecstasy. I just hoped I could come close to something as good.

Now, you must know how I even got to this point. Well when I kicked 'The Cheater' out, I got kind of lonely. I started playing around on the internet with some adult dating sites, and let me tell you, those people are a mess. It took me a while to warm up with the whole thing, because I was not like some of those women. They have pictures with all their body parts hanging out for the world to see. They were even on web camera, doing a lot of freaky things to each other. As for me, I just wanted someone to chat with. I found this one site and made me up my own profile. Shortly after, I had a few messages from some fine and not so fine men. I decided to flirt a little bit just to see if I could do it.

I sent quite a few messages back and forth to a few men. But this one in particular, DaddyLongStroke, was fine. Those muscles popping out his chest appeared to be chiseled on him. Heck yeah, I accepted his friend invite. That is when I got a chance to see why he was called DaddyLongStroke. He had one humongous penis! Looking at it had made my mouth water--and I hated sucking on my husband's.

He started off just trying to get to know me better. Then, after a few messages, he was telling me what he was going to do to me. I was actually getting wet just from reading it. After a week of him having sex with my mind, I had to meet him. I know, I know, I am technically still married. But, that relationship died a long time ago. It sure as hell didn't stop Jamal. Anyway, I decided to meet DaddyLongStroke at the Conrad downtown. We met at the bar, had a few drinks and an appetizer-- mainly because I had to calm my nerves. I have never done anything like this in my life.

It was getting late, so it was either put up, or shut time. I choose to put up. He led me to the elevator, still small talking. When the doors opened and we stepped on, all the small talk ceased. He had me pinned up against the back of the elevator, licking my neck, rubbing my titties, and my ass. I was on fire. I didn't care who was standing there when the doors opened. Evidently, he didn't either, because he continued seducing me. We went back into the hallway and down the hall to his room. Once inside his suite, DaddyLongStroke guided me towards the couch, sliding my lace thong down as we went. I had on a skirt, so it was very easy for him to do. He put his hand between my legs and started fingering the mess out of my bud and my hole. I got so wet his hand was covered in my juice. The next thing I knew he lifted up my skirt and put his tongue to work. The man was so good he almost had me speaking in tongues. He was sucking my bud so good that I was climbing up on the couch. Thankfully, he stopped before I lost my mind. But, he was far from done.

DaddyLongStroke flipped me over on the couch, so he could get a good view of my ass. He fingered me a little more to make sure I was loose. Then, he slid that big thing up in me. It hurt like hell at first. Soon, I relaxed and let him get all the way in me. He was getting me so good I thought he was going to knock my back out. I couldn't hold back my moans and screams from what he was doing to me. I didn't know the people outside those doors--so if they heard me, so what. He began smacking my ass and grabbing my hair. Funny, because that turned me on more. He was saying all types of freaky stuff to me.

"Take this dick. You like this dick in you? You like how I give it to you?" I don't think he cared one way or the other that I could not answer. My screams must have been good enough, because he came. He came so much that when he pulled out the condom was filled to the brim. Yes, I said condom. I am a clean person and would like to stay that way.

After we got washed up, he asked me if it was good. I gave him a big smile and kissed him on the cheek. I did not wait to see if he wanted me to stay. I was scared of rejection, and even more scared of him saying yes. I was sore. I straightened out my clothes and walked my sore tail back to the elevator and on to my car.

That had nothing to do with *Fantasy Girl's* but I am getting to my point. All of these adult dating sites have these advertisements for cam girls, you know webcam. Well I ignored them at first, but then I saw this one with a picture of a woman in a business suit. The woman's shirt was unbuttoned, just enough for you to get a full view of her cleavage. It didn't show the whole thing but it was more than enough for you to get the point. She had on a hat that matched the suit. It was pulled down, covering up one eye. I loved that. She looked so powerful and sexy at the same time. I was so intrigued that I clicked on the ad, which took me to the site. You had to become a member to join. Hell, I wanted to see, so I joined. To my surprise, all of the women were pretty and wearing gorgeous outfits. None of them were flaunting their naked bodies, until they went private. I went into a few girls rooms and got kicked out with a message that said get credits to join in on the private show. I wasn't quite ready for that just yet.

I had to get some sleep, because I had to get up for work in the morning. As soon as I got home the next day, and the twins were taken care of, I got back online. I looked around a little more and came across the link for interested models. I said, "What the heck," and filled out my application. I took a picture with my webcam and sent it as well. A few days later, I got an email from Erika (aka Ecstasy) and, well, you know the rest.

Now, here I am in the bookstore, looking for this Zane. I looked her up online. Come to find out, she is an erotic author. I went down the rows, trying to find her book when I got interrupted by the sales associate.

"Can I help you find anything?" a blond teenybopper asked.

"Yes, I am trying to find Zane."

"Oh yes, she is very popular. Unfortunately so popular that I sold the last copy about 20 minutes ago. But, we can order it for you. Are you looking for the new one *Sex Chronicles II*?

I started to ask if she had read it but she barely looked 18. *Sex Chronicles II*, heck what did she say the first time? I guess I was going to have to get the book before it too.

"I guess I will need the one before it as well," I replied.

"Oh good. Well you know there is another author that writes about the same type of thing. I don't want to mispronounce her name, but she did a book signing here a month ago. It was packed. The book is called *Seduction.com.* It's a sequel too."

I liked the sound of that. I needed all the skills I could find, so I ordered all four. I wanted mine in a hurry, so I paid extra. I didn't want to have to wait on their bulk shipments.

Chapter 6

I finally got my books and boy, are they good. I was sitting in the den reading *Sex Chronicles II* as the boys played outside. They ran in and out the house a few times to get something to drink but it didn't bother me. My nose was between the pages. Ecstasy really knew what she was talking about when she suggested I read this book. Forget the little 10 step how-to's in Cosmo. This book really explained it. Now, I really know that, as a woman, I can do better than just getting some mediocre sex. I need to be the seducer as well as getting seduced. It is not all just about the man getting his.

Knock, knock, knock.

Now who in the heck is beating on my door like they are the police.

Ding-dong, ding-dong

Dang, I'm coming already!

I pulled the curtain to the side to see its Jamal, Mr. Cheater himself. He stood outside, looking all confused because the locks had been changed. The boys came and went out the back door, so I did not bother to unlock the front when I got home. Did he really think I was going to let him have free roam of my house?

"What Jamal?" I said with a serious attitude. I was just getting to the good part and here he comes interrupting me.

"I came to get my boys."

"You came to do what? I haven't seen you in a month! You show up like you have it like that? Besides, it is a school night."

"I've been out of town on business. I just got back, if you must know. You the one who put me out, remember?"

"And you are the one who said I could not travel for my job, but yet you can? What the heck is wrong with this picture?"

Ole double standard having bastard.

"You said you didn't want me any more, right? So what is the issue? I didn't come to see you. I came to get my boys. Now, where are they?" Right on cue they came running into the house.

"What's up Double J?"

No, he did not just steal my name for them.

"Hey daddy!" They said in unison.

"Ya'll want to come with me to the movies?"

"Yes! Can we please Mommy?" He cut his eyes at me on that one. He hated when they asked me permission after he tells them they can do something.

"Yes, and put on your good shoes. Put the play ones up." I could see them kicked to the side of the patio door. They knew they were not allowed to walk on the carpet with them. But they could at least put the stinky things up.

The boys took off to their rooms in search of their good shoes.

"You looking good."

Huh, you talking to me?

"Thanks," came my dry reply.

"I mean it's something different about you. I can't put my finger on it but it is."

That would be good sex, sucka!

Thankfully, the boys came back downstairs and saved me from having to continue with the conversation.

He really could have cared less what I was up to. I know he was being nosey, looking for something to toss back up in my face at a later date.

"Please don't keep them out too late."

"Hey, they my boys too. I know what's best for them," Jamal said walking out the door.

And what was best was to dump them off with my sister for a week when you were supposed to be keeping them. Oh no, he couldn't dare leave him with his folks because then all the BS he feeds them would come out. He has the family thinking the boys are joined to his hip because I work, and never have time for them. He and his family can all go to hell.

Little did he know it, him taking the boys was doing me a favor. I was supposed to report back to Erika some of the things I learned. I sat down at my laptop and sent her a quick email. I thanked her for giving me a chance and for suggesting the books. I finished by telling her what I learned. I left out the part that I planned on practicing with someone first.

I started to log into the site using my screen name, ShyGirl, but the sound from my Yahoo Messenger caught my attention. It was my homeboy Devon. We both ran track together in college and have been best friends ever since. We were so cool that, one day, we were hanging out getting ready to go to his fraternity party, after the Missouri Valley Conference meet. I drank too much and passed out on his bed. I think being out in the heat all day and running in five events had something to do with it too. Instead of being pissed off or leaving me behind, he stayed in the room with me. His girlfriend was upset about it, but Devon didn't care. She always hated me being around him anyway. We would be having a Play Station tournament in his and his roommate's room, and she would be mad because I was playing the game too. I can't help it that I was the queen of Mortal Kombat and everyone was trying to take my throne.

What's up Mo? Where you been hiding?

Nowhere. Just keeping to myself is all. You know with all the Jamal stuff.

Right, but I am your homey, your big bro. You can't shut me out even though I know Jamal would love that one…smile

He was right. Jamal, hated me hanging around Devon. I was friends with Devon two years before I met Jamal. So, all his accusations about me secretly wanting Devon or vise versa fell on deaf ears.

```
Lol…It's okay. You can now
officially say you told me so.
    Naw, you been through enough. But
I did tell you to dump that loser back
in college after Homecoming remember?
```

How in the world could I forget? I sat at that game, in the freezing cold, cheering for Jamal until my voice had gone horse. He scored the winning touchdown. What did he do to celebrate? Went to a party with his football players and never even called me. But, unlike some females, I didn't wait around long. I went to the main party with my sorority sisters and had a ball. The next day I didn't hear from Jamal until about four o'clock in the afternoon. By that time, I'd heard all about his party. The football player groupies showed up and had a wet t-shirt contest. Supposedly, Jamal was all over one of them, disappearing for a few hours. Thank you caller ID. I let his no good tail go to voice mail. I ignored him for a week, but then he sweet-talked his way back in. A few weeks after we had sex, I started smelling a foul order. The more I washed the worse the smell got. I went to the clinic and they said I had a bacterial infection that it could be caused by a number of things. Yeah, and I know by who now. Back then, though, I was young and dumb and did not know that if your mate sleeps with someone else, even if they do not have a disease, you can get yeast infections and bacterial infections just from the mixing of bodily fluids and them not washing off properly.

Yeah, you told me.

Hey, gotta run. Well, at least now I can actually start back calling my best friend, instead of doing all this secret squirrel instant messaging.

Right! Smooches.

I truly did miss talking to Devon. He had an infectious laugh that I adored. Now he was a well-known DJ and in a motorcycle club. I hung out with Devon a few times when Jamal was out of town.

Well, back to logging in to this site. I had several new friend requests and a message from PlzTeachMe. I thought he looked a bit shy and nerdy at first, but he seemed really nice the few times I did talk to him. He never asked for naked pictures of me or anything like that. I figured he would be a safe candidate to practice some of my newly acquired skills on.

I sent him a message, agreeing to hook up on Friday. I included my cell phone number off my new phone. I still had my old phone, but I knew Jamal would track my calls. He had a bad habit of that. I noticed every last person in my phonebook was in his as well one day.

The idiot had taken out my SIM card and put it in his phone when I wasn't paying attention. I wondered how he knew too much about the things I was doing. He had somehow linked the text messages to his cell. I couldn't even go to the freaking mall without him knowing it. He would make sure to leave right before I did some days, just to make it so I couldn't go anywhere.

Well have fun trying to track me now, bucko. I laughed at myself every time I left the phone on my dresser. He was not about to use GPS on me.

Chapter 7

I got a message back that same evening from Ecstasy. She was impressed with what I learned. I had an appointment to go to her house and use one of her rooms for my test run on Friday evening. Thank goodness, my practice run with Earl, 'PlzTeachMe', was during the afternoon, because I had a half day of work. He said he worked on computers, so he was at my leisure.

The jerk that's about to be my ex-husband did not get the twins home until after 11:00 PM. They practically sleepwalked their entire way through school the next day. I know, because I got a note from their teacher chastising me about them needing more sleep. Now I somehow have become the bad parent in the situation.

I am sitting in my office counting down the time now. We had one boring meeting after another this morning, but that was how Friday's were. The people I work with wanted any excuse to have some catered food and do nothing all day. Me, I was still agonizing over the 10 people I had been told to let go. All but two of them were minorities and within their 90 days probationary period. One, they really had no reason for, but I have seen it several times before while working here. Instead of hiring a temp agency to send someone to work on a project, they just straight out hire someone. When the project is complete, they find a reason to fire them. Indiana is a state where you really do not have to give a reason for firing someone. Companies like mine across the state exercise this policy on a regular basis. The person does a fantastic job and the company claim something stupid, like in the first two weeks here, the new person was tardy from a break or something. That was something almost impossible to go back and prove. The letter each one gets would have dates and times on it, making you question yourself. But, in the end, there was really nothing you could do about it anyway.

"Hey, did you hear? Mike Vick is getting out today? What do you think about that?" John, one of the floor manager's, said poking his head in my office.

Did he not see me working?

"And, I should care because?"

"I mean, I thought you supported him." He said, bringing his walrus-looking body further into my office.

"Why is that?" *Cause I am black?*

"When he got his sentence all your people were on the news protesting. I thought it was going to be a riot?"

"Please explain," I said, giving this idiot my full attention now.

"You know it was the whole Black Power thing." Now John was starting to sweat. He knew he had opened his mouth and shoved his fat foot right down his throat.

"So, because some people were upset that Mike Vick got more time than a man committing involuntary manslaughter in the same week, that means that it was a Black Power uprising? It was a problem with people voicing there concerns about the penal system? You did not come to me when all the white people were on TV protesting against the animal cruelty."

"Geez Monica, you don't have to get so angry. Have a nice day," said the walrus, backing out my office.

*Once again, I am The Angry Black Woman. He
brought his fat ass in my office bothering me and I am
angry. I hate being the only black person in management.*

Yeah, I think I forgot to mention that I was the only
black person in upper management. Well technically, we
had one more in charge of Customer Service, but he did not
count. His skin may have been black, but his soul was
whiter than a member of the Aryan Nation. So I was the
one who had to hear a lot of dumb things. They thought I
spoke for the whole black race. My so-called coworkers
would ask or say the silliest things to me.

"See, a black man won the presidential election.
There is no racism here."

"There was a shooting on the news on the Eastside.
Is that close by where you live."

"Michael Jackson was from Gary. You have
relatives from there, do you know him?"

"Are you mad that Michael had kids by a white
woman, so their skin would not be dark?"

The list went on and on. I never initiated one of
those conversations. As a matter of fact, I stuck to myself
most of the time. The only other person I really spoke to
was Anita. She came from wealthy family, but got pregnant
at an early age. Her family basically disowned her. We
started working here at the same time. The only reason she

is not in management yet is because she is still finishing college.

"What did fat boy want?" Anita asked. She had seen John come out and start whispering to people.

"The usual 'ask a black person'."

"Man, the nerve of some people. I am white, and I am so embarrassed by it. I bet he is running around saying how angry you are now. The good thing is most of us know that you are one of the nicest and loyal people in the company."

"Well, at least I have you fooled," I laughed.

"So what are your plans for your half day?"

"Not too much. Take myself to lunch."

"Girl you are so boring. Well enjoy. I see you logging off already."

Now she is cool, but not that cool. I was not going to tell her that I was about to go and hook up with some guy off the internet. I planned to practice some sexy moves on him, and then use these moves on a site to bring out my inner sexuality, and bring in some extra cash.

"Later."

I watched Anita go back to her desk before I grabbed my black Prada purse, turned off the lights to my office, and locked my door. I always got a kick out of having my own door to lock. I hated sitting out there in cubical hell. Everyone was so nosey. I couldn't even go to the bathroom without folks questioning me. Now, I was the boss and could pee in peace.

Earl said he lived in the downtown area in one of the new condos. I knew exactly which ones he was talking about. I always admired them as I drove past, but I will stick to my kids having a yard to play in.

"I can't believe you are actually here," Earl said in a nerdy voice. Look, he had a Steve Urkel voice and glasses but those muscles poking out his shirt were damn sexy.

This is going to be easier than I thought.

"I can't believe I am here either. You have a very nice condo," I said, looking around.

"Would you like something to drink?"

"Do you have any fresh bottles of wine?" I was not taking anything unopened from this man. Black folks can be serial killers too. I was going to sit and watch him fill my glass to.

"I have Riesling. Is that okay?"

"Yes, I like the sweeter wines."

He poured my glass and handed it to me. I intended on sipping, but my nerves were bad. I finished it in three gulps. I waved him off on any more. That right there was enough to give me a slight buzz. Earl seemed to be as nervous as I was. Well, I did read about women needing to take charge, so I guess I better start now.

I took him by the hand and let him to his lazy boy chair in the living room. I could tell he was into the arts. He had a lot a paintings and sculptures neatly placed around the room. Not so much that it made the room look cluttered, though.

"Can you turn on the R&B XM station?" I asked. I noticed he had satellite instead of cable when I pulled up in front of his house. He responded by picking up the remote and turning to the station.

I did not buy a dancing outfit or anything like that for Earl. I knew my red lace Victoria Secret bra and thong would be enough. I pushed him back in the lazy boy chair and told him to relax. The books said to look your lover in the eyes and undress slowly. So that's what I did. I looked at him and started unbuttoning my blouse one button at a time. As I did it, I kind of rolled my body to the music. I prayed it looked sexy, and not clumsy, which was how I was feeling. I guess Earl was enjoying it, because he had a big grin on his face. When I got to the last button, I turned my back to him and let the shirt fall to the floor. I then focused on my skirt zipper, which was in the back. I pulled the zipper down as slow as I could. I didn't want to fall on my face, so I sat in his lap and leaned back on him, as I eased the skirt down my legs. I felt his penis get rock hard beneath me.

I figured since I was already in his lap I might as well try a lap dance. I basically moved my butt side to side across his penis. Then, I got bold and stood up so he could see all of my ass, with the thong going up the center.

"Oh my," he said, letting out a giggle.

I moved Earl's hands to my butt cheeks, so he could get good squeeze. He was gently rubbing and squeezing them. Then I felt something hot and moist in the crack of my ass. He was licking my ass. My cheeks clinched up, it was an involuntary reaction. I never had my ass licked before, but it was feeling good. He pulled me back until I was back in his lap and put his hand down my pants. He began playing with my kitty while he ground his penis against my ass. His fingers felt wonderful inside of me. But then it was over as faster than it started. I felt moisture against my butt cheeks so I knew he had came.

"Thank you," he said, nuzzling against my neck.

"Ummm, you're welcome," I said. What happened was not the outcome I expected. I guess I had more skills than I thought.

"You are a good teacher. You knew how to make me obey you and lick your ass without saying a word. You knew I would be a good boy."

Ok, what the hell? Obey? This joker is into some weird shit.

"Ok," I mumbled. I was trying to gather up my clothes and go.

"Mistress, is there anything else you would like me to do?" He asked, getting on his knees.

Yes, get the hell out my way, so I can go! I read about this too but it was out of my league.

"I have to leave, but remember you can't call me. I will call you. If not, you will make your Mistress very angry," I said. I hoped that would work. I picked up my purse and got the heck out of there. I could have cared less that my blouse was buttoned all wrong.

I looked at the clock on my dashboard and reasoned that I had more than enough time to go home and wash his stench off me. He was cute, but his breath was a wee bit tart.

Thankfully, my mom wanted the boys to go out to the country and fish with her, so she was picking them up from school. I would have the house all to myself. They would not be back until Sunday. She even bought them their own fishing lines and tackle box. Me on the other hand, I hated fishing. I was always the one who got stuck cleaning them. That was just plain nasty.

I rounded the corner to my house just to see Jamal's Escalade in the driveway--on my side no less. I slowed down and corrected the buttons on my blouse. There was no way I was going to have him say anything negative to me.

"Where have you been?" he asked, as if he still had the right. "I called your office and your cell."

"Does it matter? Did you care where I was when you were giving it to someone else?" I said, brushing past him.

"I am going to let that one slide. Look I have been thinking. Maybe I can deal with the traveling."

"Really?"

"Well, as long as you agree to cut back on some of your hours. I am willing to compromise with you working part time."

For a millisecond, I almost fell for it. I thought he had come to his senses.

"So let's see, I am supposed to cut back my hours and accept the fact that you cheated on me? No thanks. I will take what is behind door number three."

"What has happened to you? You used to be so nice and understanding."

"Don't you mean dumb? Those days are over. I can stand on my own. Heck, I have been doing that. Remember, it was my credit that got us this house."

"And, it was me who paid the mortgage. You sure couldn't afford it."

No thanks to your sorry ass holding me back! Punk! I was too busy killing myself helping you get your business off the ground all these years.

"Well I can sure afford it now. Thank you for being so kind and letting me take the manager position." Ha, he was ticked off when he found out I put in for it.

"Whatever Monica. I see how it's going to be. You will be missing out on me soon enough. I know it gets lonely at night under those sheets. You are too much a plain Jane for anyone to be chasing after you," he said. Jamal walked over to his truck and pulled out so fast that he almost ran over the neighbor's cat.

We will see who the plain Jane is.

I went into the house, set out a new outfit, and got in the shower. While in there, I was going over all of the new moves that I was going to try. I couldn't believe I was really going to go through with it.

Chapter 8

I didn't really expect Ecstasy to have such a big house. I knew she had to be making a lot of money, being the site owner, but this way really nice. From what I could tell, the place had to have at least four to five bedrooms. She even had security. That would be the fine man that let me in the house. I think he said his name was Ryan. I wanted to start licking on those arms of his--just yummy.

"You can use the Player's Lounge. I just had a pole installed," she said. "I don't expect you to know how to work it just yet. Climbing up it takes lots of practice. Just go ahead and get comfortable with it." Ecstasy said.

She led me past three doors, before pulling out her keys and unlocking the fourth one.

"I have a four year old. I don't want him messing around in these rooms. You can lock it back from the inside."

"Ok." That was all I could get out because I was in love with the room. It was a sex lair. From the pink, red, and black fuzzy pillows, to the heart shaped chaise. Of course, the pole was nice. It was set up in the corner, but far enough away from the wall so a girl could swing around it.

Ecstasy pointed to the computer and told me to just input my name when I was ready. Someone named Kenny would give me instructions. That was cool with me, because I wasn't too happy just dancing for a woman.

I changed into a black and red teddy. I had ordered it online from Playboy. I had some black thigh high stockings to go with it. Next, I put on my stilettos. I wore heels on a daily basis, so these weren't too bad. However, I wouldn't wear them to the club.

I added a little more gloss to my lips and took a deep breath before typing in my name. A screen, sort of like instant messenger, came up. The camera turned on and I could see myself. I was actually cute. Another web cam came on and there was Kenny.

"Hello Miss," he said.

I was surprised by his British accent.

"Are you ready?"

I gave him a nod. From out of nowhere, music started playing. I stood still a few moments with my eyes closed taking in the sound. Then, I slowly took my legs and spread them apart while I leaned back on the couch. I rolled my hips to the music, much better than my sorry lap dance I had given Earl. I moved my hands up to my breasts and cupped them, slowly caressing them. I slid my hands back down my body until I felt the silk of the stockings. I got up off the couch so he could get a full view of my body, before I unlaced the teddy and the top part opened showing my firm C-cups. Even after the twins, they maintained their perfect shape. At this point, I was really getting into it. I was ready to show him how I mastered the art of making myself reach my climax. I slid the thongs down and lay back on the chaise. I flipped the thongs off my foot and caught it with my hand in the air. I took them and made a sling shot out of them, shooting them at the monitor. I saw Kenny smile.

Using my body as a canvas and my hands as the paintbrush, I moved them seductively across my ass, fondling my breasts again. I got them nice and hard before moving on to the rest of my body. I explored every inch of myself, as if noticing it for the first time. All the while, I maintained my rhythm to the music.

Instead of sitting on the chaise seat, I sat on the back with my feet in the seat and spread my legs wide apart. With my pride and glory showing, the only thing left was to put my hand to work. I spread my shaved lips apart and toyed with my pink pearl. A few moans escaped my lips. When my juices started flowing, I stuck my middle finger in very deep. I kept fingering my bud and working my inner walls.

"Ooooh, mmmmm."

I forgot all about Kenny watching me. I was coming so hard that my body arched up off the couch, giving him a very up close and personal view. I fell back down quivering. Waves of ecstasy flowed through me.

"Miss," he said, pulling me out of bliss. "You can get cleaned up. Erika will meet you outside the door."

Did I really just do all of that for him?

I pulled myself together and cleaned up with the baby wipes that were in the room. I smoothed my hair back down and opened the door to see Ecstasy standing right in front of it.

"So I see you did learn a thing or two," she said smiling. "I knew there was something more behind those glasses."

"Thanks," I beamed. I could feel my face turning bright red. My nerves had kicked back in.

"So you ready to become a *Fantasy Girl*?"

"Are you serious? I know you have seen way better than me. I don't compare to half the girls on your site."

"Monica, look here you little vixen, you are beautiful. Most of those other girls are fake. Guys like that, but they love natural beauty even more."

I just stood there grinning like the Chester Cat from *Alice in Wonderland.*

"I will take that as a 'yes'. You can start whenever you like. My girls make their own schedule. If you are going to use my place, I have to ask that you turn that schedule in a week early, so you will have the space available."

As she was talking, a Black and Asian mixed female walked out of one of the other rooms and smiled at me. She wore a Baby Phat top and jeans. She was tall, even without the hills. She gave Ecstasy a kiss on a cheek and whispered that I was cute in her ear before heading down the stairs.

"That was Asia," she said watching my eyes follow the Amazon beauty. "See, even she approves of you."

"She is very pretty."

"Yes she is. You should check out a few of her shows. It may give you more ideas."

"I think I will just do that. Thank you so much for giving me a chance."

"Now, I have a meeting to get to. I have to fire some folks. So, please remember to follow the rules."

"Yes, ma'am." I responded like an obedient soldier. I was a few years older than her. Although I was glad to see she was about business, I was a little sad to remember that I never got to start mine.

Ryan's sexy self met me back at the door and let me out. I wondered if he had watched my show as well. I secretly hoped he had.

I could not wait to get home. With the twins gone, I could log on tonight. My office was the perfect spot for my new job. I am glad I had a chaise in the room as well. It allowed for much more movement than just sitting at the chair in front of the computer.

My cell phone rang on my way home. It was Angela. She wanted to go out and have drinks. We hadn't been out in eons, so I decided to put my new career on hold for the evening. Instead of changing into sexy lingerie when I got home, I changed into a black silky, capri jump suite, with the back out. My breast sat up on their own, so I opted out of wearing a half bra.

"Dang sis," Angela said. "I didn't know you had that in you!"

She was admiring my new outfit. I know it was nothing like I would normally wear, but I was kicking the old me to the curb, slowly but surely.

"Thank you. I got it at Be Be's."

"Well those men better watch out. I don't know if they can handle all of that."

"Whatever! With those hips of yours, I will barely be a blip on the radar," I said, bumping my hips against hers. That outfit she chose was very sexy. It was a yellow and black, mid-length dress that tied at the neck. She was working those legs.

"When are you going to ditch the glasses and get some contacts or Lasik?"

"Contacts maybe, Lasik…umm, never." I wasn't letting anyone put a laser to my eyes. Heck, I could barely see as it was. I was not about to risk being blind.

"So, are we rolling in your BMW?"

"Girl, there is nothing wrong with your Galant."

"Yes there is."

"And what is that?" As far as I knew, that car never had an issue. It's only eight months old.

"About $60,000," she responded, laughing.

"Girl you got what you can afford. When you become this big time CSI person and have your own TV show, you will have an even nicer car than mine."

I hated when she brought up money. I busted my butt to get where I was now. When I was finally comfortable in my position at Peoples Insurance, I spent part of my savings on a car that I have always wanted. Angela would get hers soon enough. I was proud of her for continuing with her education. The state job she currently had wasn't bad at all. I knew people that fought long and hard to get a government job.

"But for now, yours is fly. So, let's go ride." She snatched the keys out my hand and then ran to the garage.

Yep go ahead and drive, because you can drive home too. I am going to get my buzz on.

Chapter 9

The club was packed wall to wall. It was one of the radio personality's birthday, so they were throwing a big bash. It seemed like VIP was the only area with some room to sit down. I was willing to pay extra to have a seat. The waitress darn near beat us to the table, trying to get our drink order.

"What can I get you ladies?"

"Nuvo for me please." I had always wanted to try it. It was so cute in the bottle. Pink and sexy.

"I'll have the same. Wow, you really are coming out your shell. What happened to the wine coolers?"

"Nothing, I still drink them. But, we are in VIP baby. Time to party!"

Can You Keep a Secret?

Partying is what we did. After our first glass, we went and shook our tail feathers on the dance floor. I couldn't do all the latest dances, but I had rhythm. I few of the young boys got behind me and were trying to put it on me. I had to show them that I was no punk. I turned my back to him and started shaking my booty so hard and rolling these hips, you would have thought I was 21 again. I quickly realized I wasn't, because as soon as three songs had played, I had to go sit my tired legs down somewhere. I looked at Angela and pointed back to VIP.

"Miss, is he with you?" The security guard stopped me and asked. He was blocking the entrance to the VIP area.

"Who?" I asked. Then, I saw him. Young buck had followed me. Was he crazy?

"No." I answered and he let me past.

Sorry, Boo. It was just a dance. I am not hanging out with you all night.

I went back to our reserved table and ordered us another round. Angela would be thirsty when she came back, and not for water. I checked out the VIP area a little more. There was definitely some money up in here. I could tell by all the little groupies hanging around the men. Some of the men had three or four girls fighting for their attention at the same time.

65

"Excuse me Miss," our waitress said. "That man in the corner paid for your drinks. He would like for you to join him."

I looked back in the corner that he was sitting and saw he already had some females sitting with him. I held up my glass to show appreciation.

"Tell him thanks, but he already has enough company."

"You sure honey? He is sitting with all those football players," she said, looking at me upside my head.

"I am sure." *I'm sure as hell not about to be anyone's groupie.*

She went over there and told him something. Whatever it was had him coming in my direction.

Oh, shit. I tried looking around ready to make a run for it. I was too late. He took the empty chair next to me.

"How do you know that seat wasn't for my man?"

"Because I saw you from the moment you walked in. My name is James, by the way." He held out his hand for me to shake it. I did.

"Well it's nice to meet you James. I'm Monica."

And he is fine.

"Monica, nice. You look very sexy tonight."

I blushed. "Thank you." Why was he staring at me like that? He was looking at me so hard, it felt like he was staring into my soul.

"You have beautiful eyes. I almost couldn't tell how light they were behind those glasses, which I think are cute."

"Thank you again. Aren't some of your fellow football players going to miss your presence?" This fine man had to get away from me.

"Yeah, right. You see all the company they have? It will be two days before they notice I am gone. By the way, I am not a player."

James could have fooled me. He looked like he weighed about 220 pounds, but it was all solid muscle. His chest was huge. He reminded me of Punk from *I Love New York*, who is now with Jennifer Hudson. I was so glad Tiffany aka New York did not pick him. He was too classy for her. I am even ashamed to admit I watched the show.

"Not a player? So what are you just one of their buddies?"

"Yes and no. I used to play in college but I knew I was not going to get drafted into the NFL. I focused on my studies. Instead, I am now a sports agent."

"Impressive."

"Not as impressive as being a player. But, I like it."

We chit-chatted a while before Angela came back to the table. She took one look at James and was all smiles. She grabbed her drink and headed back to the dance floor. A few songs later, the DJ announced the last call for alcohol and put on a slow jam.

"Can I have this dance?" He asked, holding out his hand.

"Sure," came out my mouth, against my better judgment. This man was too sexy for me to be in close proximity to him.

James held my hand and led me to the dance floor. Pulling me into his chest, he put a hand on the small of my back. I took a deep breath and exhaled, like I was in a Terri McMillan novel. It felt so good being in his arms. The scent of his cologne was intoxicating. I could feel his heartbeat next against my face. He was so tall that my head rested comfortably on it. Surprisingly, his muscles weren't as hard as I thought they would be.

"Monica, what the hell do you think you are doing?" I knew that voice. I opened my eyes to see Jamal glaring at me. He had some chic on his arm, so I don't know what his problem was.

"Is there a problem?" James asked.

"Yeah, him." I said, trying to continue my dance. *Forget Jamal.*

"Hey man, that is my wife you are dancing all close up on," Jamal said, trying to size James up. Jamal worked out, but James still had about 25 pounds on him.

"Look man, it was just a dance." James said calmly.

"James, forget him. I put his cheating ass out over a month ago. Hell, he has someone with him now, so I don't know why he worried about me."

"Yeah, we working on a few issues. When the hell you start dressing like that?" He said, noticing my outfit.

"When I decided to get on with my life." By this time, I was so ready to go. This fool had the audacity to come up in here, trying to embarrass me. That was probably the chic he cheated on me with. She is a dummy to sit there, while her date was busy worrying about me.

I walked off in search of Angela. She was in the back of the club, flirting with some guy and hadn't seen a thing. Cheater was still on my heels when I found her.

"What's up?" Angela said, noticing me. "Oh, I see. Jamal, what do you want?"

"Mind your business. This is between me and my wife."

"Your wife? She put your sorry ass out." She was buzzing and did not care how loud she got. I was not going to be in the middle of a fight, so I headed outside, with Jamal on my heels.

69

"What's your problem? And, who the hell said it was okay for you to wear that outfit?" He demanded.

"You. You did not want me when you had me. So why are you bugging me?"

"I did want you. You just hard-headed."

"No, you want someone to do as you say. Those days are over." I would have started walking down the street, but my feet hurt. I was saved by something else though.

"Jamal, Jamal. I thought you said it was finally over with you two. We were going to be together, remember?" The girl ran up to Jamal, crying.

"Yeah, Jamal! What about that?" I said through gritted teeth. Like I thought, he had been messing with someone all along. I knew it wasn't a one-time thing.

He whispered something to her that she was not buying. She wanted his full attention.

"You said she didn't not know how to make a man feel good. That is why you are with me. Who wears glasses to a club anyway? They did invent contacts decades ago."

Was this heifa making jabs at me? Oh, it is on!

"You better get ya girl, Jamal, before I knock her out."

Now Jamal knew that I was quiet, but he also knew that when my buttons were pushed, I would swing first and ask questions later.

"Knock me out, bitch, please." Before she got bitch all the way out the tip of her tongue, I slapped the taste out her mouth. Jamal reacted quickly, jumping in between us.

"See, this is why I don't want you. You don't know how to act like a lady. We are in public, and you slapping people."

Was he serious? He came up to me, ruining my evening, with this little Taco Bell Chihuahua nipping at his heels. Then, she called me a bitch! Somehow, I am not a lady for slapping her. He needs to quit. I have not been in a fight in over 10 years and the last chick deserved it too. She had uttered those very same fighting words.

"Go to hell." I said. By this time, Angela had made her way out the club. When she walked over, Jamal thought twice about opening his mouth again. Angela had no problem fighting a man. She had yet to lose a fight.

"Come on," he said to his little doggie and dragged her off in the opposite direction.

"Asshole!" Angela shouted behind them.

"Let's get out of here," I said.

As we rode home, all I heard was how Angela would have beat up Jamal and his girl. She had me in tears laughing so hard. Other than him showing up, I really did have a good time.

I was still wired up long after Angela had left, so I decided to go ahead and start my new job. I stripped down to my sexy underwear and went to the site. One of the first things it asked me to do was make up a screen name. I almost forgot about that. What was it that Ecstasy called me earlier? Vixen. Sounds good to me. I typed in my new name.

`Vixen69`

The computer asked if I wanted to start free chat now. Sure, I clicked the button. My newly purchased webcam turned on. Ecstasy advised me not to use the one installed in my PC. It didn't allow for movement and couldn't zoom in very well. Plus, the resolution wasn't that great. I could see myself crystal clear on the screen. I sat there a few seconds before I realized something was missing: music. I opened up a new window and turned on a Yahoo Music station. Glad I did, because people starting coming in my room. First, it was one or two. Then, all of sudden, the whole room was packed. Ecstasy was right, they must like to see the new girls.

`Hey, pretty lady.` Someone typed.

`Hello.` I sent back.

`Where are you from?`

`Chicago.` I lied. These men ain't going to track me down.

`Show ass baby.` Someone using black font said. I remember Ecstasy said the ones with the black font did not have any credits.

`Have a little class.` Someone with green font typed. Green meant money.

I sent him a smiley face. ☺

`Share the room.` Someone else said. This must have made the one with green font mad, cause the next thing I heard was the computer voice saying, "incoming private show". The room cleared out. He and I were alone. Well, as far as he could tell, because a few seconds later, two other people voyeured in. From what I understood, the voyeurs could only watch. They could not talk back to me.

`Show me what you got, pretty lady.`
`Ok.`

`No, don't type, speak out loud.`
`Can hear you. You have a nice voice.` I forgot about that.

"Well baby," I said this is all for you. I removed my top, freeing my ample breasts, and began rubbing on them.

`They are so nice.`

"You want to suck on them?" I asked, moving closer to the monitor and pushing a button to zoom in on them.

`Ooh yes baby, let my suck on those juicy things.` I did that a few seconds and then zoomed out. I slid my hand down my thong, fingering my pearl.

`Yes baby, get it wet!`

"You want to see how wet it is?" I asked. I was really getting into this. I pulled out my hand showing him the moisture.

`I want to taste it.`

"I have something better." I slid down my thong, and opened my legs, while zooming in.

"Now eat up." When I said that, his cam to cam popped up. Cam to cam was extra. I could see his face pretending to eat me out. I even heard the slurping sounds coming from him. I had to hold back my laughter.

`You want to see it?`

"Yes, baby show me that big cock," I said, playing along.

He pulled out his average size, extra hairy, pink pecker and got to stroking away. That man was so hairy, he needed a lawn mover to trim him down.

"Yeah, that's it stroke it for me baby. Put it up in me." I lay backwards and started rocking my body towards the camera. He stroked faster and faster. We were going at it like that for a few minutes. I exaggerated my moans and groans as if he was really giving it to me.

I saw a white liquid fly out towards his camera as he ended the session.

Chapter 10

I woke up the next day to my cell phone singing to me. It was 9 o'clock in the morning, which would not have been so bad had I not stayed up to 5:00 AM on the internet.

"Hello," I said in a raspy voice. I hated my morning voice.

"Monica, hi. This is James. You know, from the club."

Yeah, and how the hell did you get my number?

"Now don't be mad, I got your number from your sister. I just wanted to make sure everything is okay. She told me that you had gone your separated ways. She also said that he was a jerk, which by the way your husband acted, I agree."

"Well, I won't be too hard on her." His voice was even sexier on the phone. "I am okay, but I was still sleeping."

"Oh I'm sorry," he lied. He was trying to catch her before she started her day. "I really wanted to know if you wanted to do lunch today."

"No, today is really not good for me. Actually, I am not ready to start dating just yet."

"It's not a date. It is just two friends hanging out."

With a body and the looks you have, you could never be just my friend. He seemed nice enough, but I still was not ready.

"Sorry, I have to pass."

"Well I am very sorry to hear that. I tell you what. You have my number now, so call me if you ever want to just talk."

Talk, ha! If you only knew that all those men I helped get off last night, I pretended they were you. I was cumming for you.

"Ok. I'll store your number in my phone," I answered and then hung up.

I was tired. I rolled back over in my satin sheets and fell back to sleep. I ended up having six private shows and was in the nude chat room for over and hour. The time flew by. I had to force myself to get offline because of the time.

One thing with the internet was that time zones were not a factor. Some of those men were in different countries.

I woke up from a dreamless sleep three hours later with my stomach growling out of control. I headed down to the kitchen looking for a cure. I found it: some bacon, eggs, grits, and toast. When I was done, my stomach thanked me by letting out a burp. I took a shower, got dressed to do some grocery shopping, and checked the mail. I almost did a back flip. I had just met with my lawyer on Monday and here I was looking at some divorce papers. Now all I had to do was to get Jamal sign them. I guess it helped that I paid her all at once, instead of using her payment plan option.

"Hello," Jamal answered with a serious attitude.

"Hey, we need to talk," I said, using my professional voice. The one I reserve for work.

"What about now?" He said it like I call him on a regular basis or something.

"This needs to be face to face. Do you have time today?"

"Not really, but I will make time," he said. The only thing he planned on doing was sliding back up in the woman lying next to him. However, Jamal was curious to see what Monica was up to. He was shocked to realize that woman he was checking out was his wife at the club. That outfit she had on was very sexy. Just nothing he ever expected to see on his wife.

"How about an hour?"

"Fine. Are the boys up yet?"

"They are fishing."

"Fishing?" He could not stand her country-ass family. They moved up north and brought the country with them.

"Yes, you know they love it."

"But, I planned on hanging out with them today."

"Well you have to plan for another day now." That was so like him to claim he wants them when he knows they are not around.

"Hey I have to go," he said, hanging up. Jamal's conversation had stirred the woman next to him awake. She overheard my voice. Apparently, this chic wanted his attention so she started giving him head.

I didn't miss the slurping sounds in the background. Good for him. More reason to sign these papers. I turned on some music and began straightening up the house. It was far from messy, but the boys PSP's, action figures, and socks were lying around. The place could stand a little dusting too.

I had just put in a load of laundry, when I heard Jamal's truck pull up. I looked out the window and saw that his little doggie was in the passenger seat.

Oh, no the hell he didn't.

"What is she doing here?" I snapped, as I snatched open the front door. At least he was smart enough to leave her in the truck. I might have had to finish what she started last night.

"I am giving her a ride. Now what is this all about?"

"I want a divorce," I said, handing him the papers. "You have already moved on so just sign the dang papers and be on your way."

Jamal snatched the papers out my hand and started looking them over. He had to admit, I didn't leave him much to complain about. I only wanted the house and child support. He would gladly pay child support. He wasn't about to keep the boys. We were interrupted by a knock on the door.

"What?" I said, snatching open the door. I just knew it was that heifer and I was ready to let her have it.

"Hi, Mrs. Taylor, are the twins here? Can they come out?" A light skinned, nine year old with green eyes asked.

"No, Lil' Tony, they are gone for the weekend." I said, changing my tone. Without another word, the boy took off running back to his yard. One thing about this neighborhood there was a lot of mixed couples. All well educated, professional black men married to white women. We used to be the only all black couple in the neighborhood, that is, until I put Jamal out.

I turned around and there was Jamal, looking at me like I was crazy.

"See, that is why I signed this. You snatched open the door ready to act out. This is not the ghetto, and you should behave better." I've changed and he did not like it one bit.

"Well thanks," I said, taking the papers and leading him to the door. I hope he doesn't think we are going to have to wait the usual 90 days and have a court date. My lawyer also had a petition in there to waive the final hearing, as long as we both agreed. His signature was not required on that page, so I felt no need for him to see it.

I picked up the house phone to call my lawyer's office to leave a message. Much to my surprise, the office was open.

"Hello, Mrs. Taylor," the secretary said.

"Hi, my husband signed the divorce papers. I wanted to know when would be a good time to drop them off."

"Well, I will be here until 2:00 this afternoon, or you can drop them off on Monday."

I looked at the time. It was 1:30, just enough time for me to make it downtown. Glad I was already dressed.

"Thank you. I will be there shortly." I said, hanging up the phone. I found my purse, car keys, and hit the highway.

Chapter 11

Now, when I say my lawyer was quick, I meant she was quick. I turned the papers in on Saturday. She took them to the judge on Monday. On Wednesday, I had a certified copy of my divorce decree in my hands. This would be why Jamal was blowing up my cell and work phone at this moment. He got his set of papers as well. I was not about to answer his calls. I already knew he was ticked. He had called me later on that same evening, saying he changed his mind and would fight it with his own lawyer when we went to court.

Tough break sucka.

"What is the focused look for?" Anita said, poking her head in my office.

"Trying to get these reports together before this next meeting in Washington DC."

"Aren't you sick of those boring things? I mean, how much more can the big wigs complain with about the new health care changes? Anything is better than the one we have now."

"Yeah, try telling that to the bigwigs. It isn't affecting them, so why do they care? It really is not an issue for me right now either. But, for my other family members, this health care bill is a very big deal. Wish I could chat more, but I have to get these done so they will have them while I'm gone. I don't plan on having anybody call me every ten minutes while I am gone," I said, never raising my head up from the spreadsheet I was working on.

Earlier, Angela put up a fuss, but she agreed to keep the boys again for my trip. Unlike the other times, I would only be gone four days instead of a full week. My flight was leaving this evening at 7:00, so I would be in D.C. and refreshed for the first meeting at 8:00 in the morning. I was basically there as the eyes and ears of our company, this time. Not that they would have listened to anything I had to say anyway.

I worked until four, got my reports emailed, then zipped home to get the boys. I half expected Jamal to be waiting at my doorstep when I arrived. I was glad he wasn't.

The boys were in the dining room, finishing up their project when I walked in. You might as well say the dining room was the study room, because it had been over two years since we all sat down together and ate as a family. I would still cook my fancy meals that I loved, but with Jamal always working late, his plate used to just sit in the microwave. There was no need for just me and the boys sit at the table, not for them to gobble it down in ten minutes.

"Hey babies." I sang, walking in the room.

"Eww mom, we are not babies any more." Jaylen said.

"Yeah mom, we are almost in double digits now," added Jayden.

"You are my babies and you will always be," I said, kissing them both on the cheek. I'm sure if their friends were around, they would have wiped it off.

I left them to their project and went up stairs to change into some more comfortable traveling clothes. I loved that the camp gave them projects to work on. They focused on keeping the boy's minds busy during the weeks of summer. Next year, I wouldn't need the camp, because their school was changing from traditional into year round. I ditched the business suite for a DKNY blouse, Calvin

Klein slacks, and lower heeled shoes. The boys were done with their homework by the time I came out my room.

"Don't worry about a snack. I will stop by Subway. Now, go get your bags and come on." I had double checked their bags and put my luggage in the car, before I left for work this morning.

I made it to the gate barely five minutes before they started making the first boarding calls. I prayed to not get stuck next to another elderly lady. The last trip, I sat next to one who talked my ear off. I didn't care about her six cats or her ailments. I did feel bad about her kids not coming to visit her anymore, though.

Today must have been my lucky day, because the flight was not full, and no one was sitting next to me. I put up my bag and took the window seat. I dozed off before the plane was in the air.

Good thing my job was picking up the tab for the trip. They had me staying at the Four Seasons, which was the same hotel where the meetings were being held. The rooms were almost $400 a night! I got settled in my room and called Devon. It felt so good to actually call my best friend whenever I wanted to again. I hated having to instant message him all the time.

"What's up Baby Girl?" He said, answering the phone.

Can You Keep a Secret?

"I am letting you know I made it safe and sound."

"Well, that's good to know. But you were supposed to call before the plane took off," he said in a fatherly tone.

"Sorry, I was running late and fell asleep before we got off the runway. Anyway, guess what?"

"What?"

"I am officially a divorced woman!"

"Oh, we are going to celebrate when you get back."

"That's fine with me. It's a date." But I had planned on celebrating a little sooner than that. I started talking online to a few men in the area over a week ago. I used my normal adult dating site and not *Fantasy Girls*. There was no way in the world I would date any of those men.

"Well go ahead and relax. I was riding my bike when you called and had to pull over. I am on my way downtown."

"Ok, be careful. Smooches."

I ordered room service and then grew anxious sitting in the room. I headed downstairs to the bar. I figured if I drank a glass of wine, it would help me sleep better. I was really nervous about the meeting in the morning. The outcome could result in big changes within the company. I had a feeling my job would be secure, but with the way the economy was going, who knew what tomorrow would bring. I had more than enough saved to get me by for at least six months, though without dipping into my 401K or savings bonds.

"What can I get you?" The bartender asked. He was overly flamboyant, like most of the gay men I knew and enjoyed meeting.

"A glass of Ice Wine please."

"I woman with taste I see," he said, pouring my glass.

I winked at him and took a sip. The sweet taste was heaven to my throat.

"So, what's a beautiful woman like you doing drinking alone?" A voice said behind me.

I looked up to see a nice looking, mid 30's, white man with a dark tan, standing behind me.

"What makes you think I am alone?" I said, smiling.

"Because you only ordered for yourself."

"Point taken."

"You mind if I join you?"

"Sure, why not."

"I am Edward by the way," he said, offering me his hand.

"I am Monica."

"What brings you to D.C. Monica?"

You sure are freaking nosey.

"Meetings."

"I see. You too, huh? I am here for the same thing."

"Well, I hope it was not as boring as the last few I have been too."

"I hope not either. I heard the speaker was a pompous ass," he said, leaning in a little to close for my comfort.

"Is that right? Well I will know soon enough." I knew enough from working at my office not to get caught up in those types of conversations. The next thing you know if you did comment, you would be confronted as if you were the one who brought the whole thing up. Changing the conversation, I said, "So where are you from?"

"New York and you?"

"Indiana."

"Indiana? I am surprised. You have a bit of a southern accent. Not strong, but it is definitely there."

"I moved up to Indiana from Mississippi in high school."

I finished my drink, waving the bartender off from refilling my glass. I wanted to get away from this man. He was too nosey and arrogant for my liking. Kind of like most of the upper management males I ran into. I pulled out my card to pay, but he insisted on covering my tab. I thanked him and headed back to my room. I feel asleep watching

Hawthorn, Jada Pinkett Smith's new show. The series was actually pretty good. I am grateful TNT picked it up.

Chapter 12

So, there I was, in a boring meeting, trying not to fall asleep. Had I not been the only black female, I probably would have succumbed to sleep. We have already had three people speak, each saying that they wouldn't be long. Forty-five minutes later, they finally finished. I am not a fan of energy drinks, but I was going to try one on our next break. I had to do something. Otherwise, my forehead was going to smack the table in front of me.

I was almost a goner until they announced the CEO of the New York office. Wouldn't you know it, it was the man from last night. It may have been my imagination, but it seemed as if he was looking directly at me while he spoke. He was an excellent speaker, very animated. He had my undivided attention.

Bzzzz, bzzzz, bzzzz I almost jumped out my chair. It was my cell phone vibrating against my skin. I slid it under the table to make sure it wasn't anything important. It was a text message.

`I can't wait to taste you.` I blushed. It was from the guy I was meeting up with tonight. There where two more messages behind it.

`To lick your inner sweetness,` was what the next one said.

`And make you cum all over me.` I was smiling so hard, I know I looked like an idiot. Thankfully, Edward had mercy and called for a 10-minute break. I took off to the bathroom to compose myself. I never had anyone talk to me that way, let alone send me messages like that. I was getting hot just from reading them. I splashed some water on my face, gathering myself, and then headed back out.

"Something have your attention?" Edward asked. He almost made me jump out of my skin. He must have come from the men's bathroom, because he walked up right behind me.

"Excuse me?" I said.

"During the last part of the meeting, you seemed to be smiling to yourself an awful lot."

"Is there some sort of law against it?" I questioned. *Why the hell are you all up in my face?*

"No, just thought it was something you would like to share. By the way, you look nice today." Now, with that he got a huge smile from me. I had tried out one of my newer suits today. I found one that was made especially for my shape. It kind of looked like the one Ecstasy wore on her site. Of course, I kept my top buttoned. Now, I look like I belong on *CSI Miami* instead of on the older *Law and Order* series. "I must admit, I do love that my fellow sista's have style."

"What the…" but he was already gone. Sista's? What the heck was he talking about? He did have a serious tan going on, but he still looked white to me. His head was shaved bald so that was no help.

That last comment had me eyeballing Edward the rest of the day. I was so focused on him, that I could barely eat my lunch without taking peeks at him. Our meeting finally ended around 3:00 that afternoon. By then, I was so ready to get away. Those stuffy men were on my last nerves. I never heard so much President Obama bashing in my life.

I hopped on the elevator, leaned up on the back wall, and closed my eyes.

"Surely, I didn't bore you that much." I knew who it was before I even opened my eyes.

"Edward, of course not. It was the other three before you." I answered candidly.

"I like your honesty. They were rather boring to me as well."

"About your sista comment earlier…"

"Well, here is my floor. I would love to see you around dinner time," he said, cutting me off.

"I have plans sorry."

"Lucky guy," he said, letting the door close to the elevator.

This Edward dude was confusing me by the minute. I had a trick for him. I am going to Google him as soon as I get out the shower.

I was still sitting in my bath towel when I sat in front of my laptop. I typed in his name and pulled up some information.

CEO to one of the largest insurance companies in the United States. I knew that information, so I clicked on another link. Making the Forbes 500 List for the 5th year in a row…the company is headed by CEO Edward Hamilton, one of the few minorities ever to hold this position. His mother is African American and Irish, while his father was of European descent...

Go figure. So he was a brotha. Now, I know some people would say that makes him more white than anything, but not in the black community. We still hold onto that one drop of blood. He is a black man in my book. But I still was not going to dinner with him. I looked up the directions for this Jazz Club that I was supposed to be meeting my fling at. It was actually not as far as I thought. Even though I would be taking a cab, I still liked to know where I was going.

I decided to eat at the restaurant downstairs before I left for my rendezvous. I had to admit this hotel had great food. My steak was perfect. Well done, but not burnt. It was so tender I really could have used a butter knife to cut it. The staff was wonderful as well. I didn't feel rushed at all, which is normally what happens when I eat alone. I guess they figure I am alone with no one to talk to, so there is no reason to linger.

I left my waiter a hefty tip and headed back to my room. I wanted to brush my teeth and spray on some perfume before I left. I passed Edward on my way up. I just smiled and kept going.

I hope not every cab in the city drove like this. This man was throwing me all over the back seat. And, I was wearing my seat belt. He was swerving all through the traffic the whole time. I kept reassuring the cab driver that I was not in a rush. He either did not listen or did not understand me. It had nothing to do with him being from Africa, but everything to do with the extra thick bulletproof glass separating us.

By the time he pulled up in front of the club, I thought I was going to have motion sickness. I got out the car and tipped him. He pealed off in search of his next victim. The club looked very small from the outside, almost like a hole in the wall. Surprisingly, there were several people outside waiting to get in. I walked over to them, taking my place in line. I sent a text to my fling, letting him know I was there. He sent one back saying he was a few minutes away and to find us a table.

The place was very nice on the inside. Not at all small as it appeared from the outside. I chose a table in the far right corner of the club. Not like I really had a choice, the club was packed. There was a local musician performing, and he was good.

At sat there a few minutes, enjoying the music, and sipping on my drink. I saw someone very familiar heading in my direction. It was Edward. *What the heck was he doing here?*

"Is this seat taken?" He asked.

"Not at the moment, but I am waiting on someone," I answered. He needed to leave before my date showed.

"You mean you aren't ShyGirl?"

I almost choked on my drink. This cannot be right. This had to be some sort of joke.

"There is no way I could have mistaken those pretty brown eyes. I knew it was you the moment I saw you sitting at the bar. I wanted to tell you, but I didn't want to scare you off."

Finally finding my voice I said, "I think I need to leave."

See I had a picture of myself on the site. It was a discreet profile in which you had to be my friend in order to see it. He on the other hand had body pictures, and what a lovely body it was. I even knew he had an eagle tattoo on his back right shoulder and that his member curved to the left. This was too dang weird.

"Monica, don't leave. It's okay. Let's at least enjoy the evening," he said. At that moment, someone brushed past bumping into him. She apologized and said she was looking for a pay phone. It was strange because some man was fast on her heels, but he got side tracked by another woman stepping in front of him. He seemed to care less about the woman he was following the moment.

"Okay," I said, sitting down. "Hold on. What about those messages you sent me earlier? How the heck did you do that when you were in front of us speaking?"

"I sent those messages on the break we had right before I began speaking. I guess with the bad reception we get in the conference area it was delayed. Believe me, I did not plan for you to get those in the middle of me speaking. But, I must admit, I enjoyed the look on your face."

"That was just evil," I said glaring at him. "But, I guess we are both here now. Go ahead and take a seat."

He slid into the seat next to me. His armed bumped mine, sending a shock wave through my entire body.

"You cold?" He asked, noticing me shiver.

"No, I'm okay. I just need another drink." I answered.

He caught the waitress walking past us again. "Umm, the lady will have?"

"A long island ice tea." I needed something a lot stronger than what I was currently sipping on.

"And, Liquor 43 for me please, thank you."

"So, do you come here often?" I asked. I had to say something.

"Only on business trips."

"Well, do you always take your women here?"

"Believe it or not, this is my first time actually following through with someone I chatted with on the site. I really had no intentions of hooking up with you. But, once I saw you in person, I had to. The reason I never met with any of the other woman was because I dated on the internet years ago, and every woman I met looked nothing like the pictures I saw. They were either 40 or 50 pounds heavier. Or, it was really their cousin on the picture instead of them..."

"Why does someone who looks like you use the adult site anyway. You would think women would be throwing themselves at you."

"I could ask you the same. The fact is I work a lot. I've tried to date here and there, but I'm not ready for a relationship right now. My ex fiancé and I went through a bad breakup, and well, I just don't really feel like dealing with anyone else on that level right now."

"Good enough for me," I was leaving that conversation alone. I didn't want to get into my personal life at all.

After a few more drinks, we sat there laughing and joking about some of the other people at our meetings. We wondered how some of them even got into upper management. A few looked like they couldn't manage themselves out of a paper bag.

I finally relaxed and was really enjoying myself. Edward relaxed too. He rested his hand on my thigh. Before long, he was inching it up further. I squirmed a little, but did not remove his hand. It was dark. No one could see up under the table. Besides, all the other tables were in front of ours. Edward pushed my skirt up and moved my thongs to the side. I let out a soft moan. He started gently rubbing my bud with his index finger. It wasn't long before my juices were flowing.

"Let's go outside," Edward whispered. He left money for the waitress and led me toward the door. Once outside, he pulled me to the side of the building, opposite the parking lot and away from the street light. He pushed me against the wall and dropped to his knees. He put his head under my skirt and did exactly what he said. He licked my sweetness and made me have an orgasm all over his face.

The liquor giving me courage, I grabbed his penis and pulled him towards me. I took it in my mouth and sucked it like a pro. This was the second one I had ever had, but I worked it like I had done thousands. Unlike Jamal, he did not try shoving it down my throat. He let me do as I pleased. He was moaning just as loud as I had been while he was pleasing me.

"I need to feel the inside of you," he said.

He slid on a condom as I lifted my leg, wrapping it around his waist. He slid inside of me. His member was bigger than I thought, but I took it. He began giving it to me, right there against the side of the building. I was taking it like a champ. I had to admit, I had wanted him just as bad as he wanted me.

"Cheryl, I am not going to chase you all night!" I heard someone yell. It didn't stop our rhythm though.

"Then don't Kevin!" The woman replied back. She yelled just as Edward came drowning out his moans. We lay against the wall, spent from our freak session. I pulled down my skirt while he pulled up his pants.

"Do you hear that?" I whispered to him. It sounded like gurgling sounds. We came from around the corner. The man released her neck when he saw us.

"Are you okay?" I asked, running over to her.

"I am fine. We just talking," she said, trying to catch her breath.

Woman are you insane? This man was trying to choke the life out of you and you are calling it talking. Okay, stay here. Let him kill you, then.

"If you say so," I answered, instead of saying what I really wanted. Cheryl, I guess that was her name, took off back inside the building. Kevin started walking away from the club.

"That was crazy." I said to Edward.

"Yes, but without her wanting help, there was nothing we could do."

I was feeling weird again. I just humped one of my company's CEO's. I had a reason for not messing with anyone I had to see the next day. I guess he was feeling my apprehension because he suggested we ride back in separate cabs. That way no one would notice us going back into the hotel together. I was fine with that.

Chapter 13

I went through another long, boring day of meetings the next day. I was glad that round didn't start until 9:00 AM because I had drank a little more than I intended the night before. Edward smiled in my direction a few times and that was it. No more text messages or elevator conversations.

When the day was over, I did my usual, headed straight to my room. I had no plans for the evening, other than reading another good book that was referred to me.

I had a few hours to spare before diner so I got on *Fantasy Girls* to make a few men' s dream come true. When I was online, I actually felt as if I was my alter ego, Vixen69. I was bold and daring with the men when I was her. I had no problem telling them what I wanted to be done to me and egging them on with their fantasies. I never knew how enjoyable it was to experience an orgasm over and over again. Those men did not care if I really came, as long as I made a lot of noise doing it and they got theirs as well.

One thing I found that was absolutely hilarious was when a man's credits ran out before he came. We would instantly get disconnected and a few minutes later, they will show back up ready to finish themselves off. The broke men were funny too. They would beg and beg to see some skin. I mean come on they should have been happy to see me sit around in my sexy underwear, but I entertained them as well. I gave them a dance sometimes, which the whole chat room would enjoy.

I was online up until 7:00, that was when my stomach told me it needed nourishment. I hopped into the shower, got dressed and headed downstairs for diner. The restaurant was full of mostly my coworkers from the conference. I preferred to eat alone, but a group of eight was calling me over to them. There were six men and two women. Edward was among them. I could have sworn one of the women rolled her eyes at me when I sat down.

Can You Keep a Secret?

Don't worry heifer, I don't want none of these men. Well maybe one, but I already had him. You can have the rest.

Not a very big talker, I remained quiet most of the meal. I only spoke when someone asked me a direct question. Bill Worthington ran our Michigan office and was commenting on my resume.

"Monica, I am so surprised you are only a Human Resources Manager. I see your name attached to so many files that you would think you were the assistant VP or something."

It was strange how I was the only HR person at all conferences and meetings I have attended.

"Well, I am sure it's just her name attached to the all user emails," Patricia Zimmerman chimed in. That was the heifer that rolled her eyes at me.

"No, I was correct in what I said. The email may come from someone else, but I always look to see who actually did the work on a project. Way to go Monica. I would love to have you on my team. If you ever think about coming to Michigan, make sure you look me up." He said, shutting Patricia up.

"Thank you," I said. "Well I did get my Master's in business management, but of course without the experience I fell back to my BA, which was in HR."

"Impressive." Came the replies from everyone else at the table.

"Well, I want to know where you go shopping. I love your outfits," said Ann Gable. She was the other lady at the table. That was the first time I had heard her say a word.

"Before we leave I will get your business card and fill you in. Right now, I don't want to bore the men. Especially after the last speaker we had."

"Yes, please spare us," someone else said causing the table to erupt with laughter. The last meeting of the day had everyone ready to commit suicide. I saw a few of them nod off a few times. Some even faked important calls from their home office.

I ended up sitting at the table with them for over two hours. I needed to make a call and check on my boys, so I was the first to excuse myself.

"Hey Angela."

"Hey girl. How is DC? Any fine men there?"

"Yes, there are, but that is not what I am here for." I was not about to tell her I just got banged by one outside a club last night. "Where are my babies?"

"In the other room, playing the video game. You know that is what the kids do now days. Hold on I will get them."

"Hey mom. You okay?" Jayden asked.

"Yes."

"Hey mom. What is DC like?" Jaylen asked. Jayden had gotten his answer and passed the phone to his brother.

"It is nice. Lots of people. You would be shocked to see that there are homeless people just blocks away from the White House."

"Really, well take a lot of pictures. Hey Jayden, it's my turn!" He said dropping the phone on the counter. I could hear them fussing in the background.

"Girl, they are crazy." Angela said, picking back up the phone.

"That is why they have their own rooms. Twins yes, acting alike, not even close. Jayden is just like his dad, selfish to the core."

"Maybe he will grow out of it."

"I doubt that. Look someone is at my door. I will talk to you later." I hung up the phone. I had no clue who that could be.

I looked through the peephole to see Edward standing on the other side. I wondered what he wanted. I barely got the door open before he rushed me, kissing me hard. He kissed me like I was a lover he hadn't seen in weeks.

"Edward?" I wanted to ask what was going on but he silenced me with more kisses. He kissed me all the way back to my bed. His hands were all over my body. He slid my pants down tossing them to the floor. My shirt went flying next, followed by my bra and panties.

"You are so sexy," he murmured, before diving between my thighs.

"Oh, mmmm," was all I could say. He turned his body around on the bed and his penis was dangling in my face. I guess he wanted me to lick on it, so I did. I only thought people did this in porno films. The faster he licked me the harder I licked on him. He made me cum not once, or twice, but three times in this position. He then flipped me over and put my hands on the headboard. He came at me from behind and gave it to me doggie. We were making so much noise I knew the people in the room next door had to hear us. Thankfully, it wasn't anyone from our group.

"I want to cum on your ass," he said, pulling out. He took off the condom and released warm liquid all on my back. I truly think he was trying to turn me into a freak. I loved everything he did to me.

"Thanks baby," he said, kissing me again. He put his clothes back on and left.

What the hell was that?

I played his game the next day as well. Hey, I
wanted a fling and that's exactly what he gave me. During
the day, it was strictly business as usual and at night, it was
fun. When he wasn't turning me out, I even managed to
sneak in a few hours on *Fantasy Girls.*

I was so happy to be done with the conference that I
sang all the way to the airport. I ignored the taxi driver's
terrible driving and even left him a nice tip. As I waited for
my plane, I received a text from Edward.

Be safe and thank you for these
wonderful few days.

You are welcome. I sent back.

Can we keep in touch?

Sure why not? I didn't see any problem with
that. I was not going to travel to get a piece though. It was
what it was, a fling.

Ok, talk to you soon.

They were calling my row to board, so I picked up
my carry on and boarded the plane. I turned off my cell and
got comfortable in my seat. Once again, I was counting
sheep before the plane took off.

Chapter 14

"When I said for you to call me when you felt like talking, I did not realize it would be this long of a wait," James said, teasing me.

It was Monday and I was on my lunch break. I decided to be nice and give him a call. Plus, I wanted to hear his deep sexy voice.

"Well, I am a busy woman. I marked it down in my calendar a few days ago to call you at this time today." I joked back.

"I am so glad you stick to your schedule," he laughed. "But seriously, how have you been?"

"Well, I just came back from a business trip and I am divorced now."

"Divorced? That was fast. From the way your sister made it seem I thought it was going to be something long and drawn out."

"Not with the lawyer I had. I was actually shocked Jamal signed the papers. Then again I guess he had to prove it to his new woman that he was really over me."

"Yeah, that whole thing at the club confused me. He was questioning us dancing, yet he had another woman with him. What a jerk."

"It's done and over with now. I am free of him and his male chauvinistic ways."

"So, now it is okay for us to go on a date."

Who said that? I just wanted to talk.

"I told you, I am not ready for that yet," I answered, switching from my playful tone to a more serious one.

"Not even just diner?"

"Nope. Look, my lunch is almost over. I have to go." I said, disconnecting the call.

I have no idea why going out with him was such a big deal to me. I guess I was not ready for all that. I no longer had the desire to have to answer anyone. I was enjoying my freedom.

Anita was all smiles when I came back to the office.

"What's the big secret?" I asked.

"I don't know, you tell me," she said, looking in the direction of my office.

I looked in the direction of my office and saw a vase full of beautiful lilies. I was confused, because I was quite sure Jamal was not sending me flowers after all the hateful messages he had left me. He had done far worse in the past. And I had I never received a freaking a dandelion.

Anita was on my heels as I walked into my office.

"So who are they from?"

"Dang Miss Nosey, can I open up the card?" Before I got a chance, she snatched it out the vase and read it out loud.

"Monica, thank you for gracing us with your presence. I am glad I had the chance to meet you. Edward," she looked at me all confused. "Well that was rather boring. I was sure it was something juicy. Look, I can't be the only one of us having sex. You need to get a man girl."

"Well I think it was very sweet," I answered, hiding my smile. I could read between the lines. That was very nice that he thought of me the morning after. "And I will just continue to get my sexual gratification by listening to your stories."

Why the heck was she worried about who I am sleeping with? That is my own secret, and I am going to keep it.

"Okay Miss Boring, I will get out of your face for now. At least the flowers are beautiful."

When Anita left, a few more people stepped in to comment on them. I gave them less information than I had given Anita. You would think they would be used to my tight-lipped ways by now. I never gave my coworkers personal information when they asked. The most they even know about my family is the from one picture frame that I have at my desk. And, you have to be sitting on my side to see it. Only Anita knows about mine and Jamal's divorce. I doubt if she says one word to anyone else, being that I am the keeper of all of her secrets.

Five o'clock, thank you Jesus! I was suffering from jet lag really bad. I was tired and irritable. I should have taken today off, but we had a mandatory meeting. The upper management were starting to get stricter with the employees. I had to listen to them go over their new list of things the employees could not do. They way they ranted and raved, it wouldn't be long before a Port a Potty was installed at each cubicle.

On a good day, it only took me 20 minutes to get home. Today was not one of those days. I sat on I70 for 45 minutes, creeping along at 10 miles per hour, just to find out the accident wasn't even on our side of the highway. A semi truck's cargo door was flung open. Apple boxes were spread across the westbound traffic lanes. A freaking gaper's delay (commuter speak for traffic jam), and now as I round the corner to my house I see a black Cadillac with 26 inch rims sitting in the dang driveway.

What the heck does he want now? I just want to relax.

"Monica! I did not agree to this!" Jamal screamed, walking towards me.

"Yes you did. You signed the divorce papers. I didn't forge your name."

"Well I changed my mind. What happened to us going to court?"

"No need to. You signed it. What is the issue?" *Was it because I beat you to the punch?*

"Whatever, Monica," he said my name with disgust. "This is not over."

"Are you insane? Do you need some medication? You got what you wanted. You got rid of the wife that was not the person you wanted to be with. Remember, I am not Susie the Happy Homemaker."

By this point, he was really starting to freak me out. I really did not know what the problem was. I saw one of our neighbor's walk outside. I needed a diversion, quick.

"Hey Jennifer!" I said, waving to her.

Jennifer took this as her cue to run over to my yard. She bounced across the street in her extra tight jeans and tank top. Her fake boobs were propped up on display as usual.

"Hi, Monica! I have been meaning to get with you. I am having a Pampered Chief party this weekend and would love it if you would come. Oh hi Jamal." Jennifer never cared for Jamal, though. She saw his cheating ways every time Monica went out of town. She could not believe he had that woman in the house for almost an entire week. Jennifer didn't know the whole story, but from what she could tell, he was no longer staying there. Good riddens!

Jamal was not about to wait around for them to finish talking. He stomped back to his truck and pulled off.

"Why sure," I said, watching him back out the driveway. "I read the email you sent out about it."

"Okay great. The food will be delicious. I was thinking about doing a wine tasting as well."

"That sounds fantastic. Well, I have to handle a few things so I will talk to you later. You know I just got back in town," I quickly inserted the key and left her standing outside. Jennifer was nice, but she was nosey. The entire housing addition would know all of my business if I told her anything.

When we first moved into the neighborhood a few years back, Jennifer was one of the main women trying to flaunt themselves in front of Jamal. She would see Jamal outside and run over to speak with him. I even caught her outside gardening in her booty shorts a few times. She should have focused more on taking herself to the gym than showing all that cottage cheese to Jamal. She soon learned that Jamal loved his beautiful black woman and backed off. Well at least that's what I like to think.

I went into the house and kicked off my heels. I could have sworn I heard my feet say "thank you". I turned on the news and sank into the soft cushions of my couch, ready to take a short nap. I could feel the heaviness in my eyelids taking over.

"Hi Mom!" Double J said together, busting in the back door.

"Can we make a sandwich?" Jaylen asked. He was already taking out the peanut butter and jelly.

"Sure," I half mumbled. "How was camp?" Not that I really cared. Today it was just an automated response.

"Fine!" Came their usual response.

"Can we go back to the tree house when we are done?" Jayden asked.

"Sure, just clean up your mess." I realized that a nap on the couch was not a very good idea, so I headed up stairs.

Chapter 15

I woke up about an hour later, feeling refreshed. I checked on the boys, who were back in the house playing the Wii. I tried talking to them for a while, but the game had their attention. So, I headed back up stairs to my office. As bad as I wanted to log into *Fantasy Girls*, I decided to wait until the boys fell asleep. I could see it now, I would be getting a customer all hot and ready to explode and one of them will bang on the door, asking me a silly question like can they get something to drink. The boys knew that they did not have to ask, but just because I was busy, they would do it anyway. I realized that no matter how low I turned the microphone down on the site, the men still seemed able to hear me. I learned that lesson, while answering the phone for Angela one day when I was online. I had on my earpiece, so I thought nothing of it. I just turned down the volume, kept toying with my client, and talked to her. The next thing I saw was.

Are you talking to another woman?

Ask her to come join you.

I would love to see you do each other.

I abruptly ended the call with Angela. But for the rest of the show, that was all he wanted. I quieted him up once he came and ended the show. So for now, I will stick with checking my email.

I had one from Ecstasy. It was an invitation to her new club, Club Secrets. She wanted all of her employees to attend and mingle. It was an elite club with a dining area and private rooms. Her email assured me that I did not have to work her private rooms. I was psyched to say the least. This young woman had some serious business sense about her. Heck yes, I would attend.

The rest of my email was mainly junk mail, so I deleted it. I went to my adult dating page and had a few messages, but not from anyone I was interested in. I surfed the internet a little more until I was overcome with boredom. I decided to research a little more about temporary agencies. It was still my dream to own one someday. The hard part would be building a client base.

Getting the employees would not be hard at all, with the economy the way it was.

By the time I was finished, it was late into the evening. It was time to get the boys to bed. To my surprise, they had both already showered by the time I went to check on them.

"We already showered," Jayden said, not looking up from the game.

"I know. I can smell the soap, instead of two funky puppy dogs now." I said. I always wondered why kids smelled like puppies when they came from outside.

"Can we get ten more minutes, Mom?" Jaylen asked.

"Okay, but after that. It's lights out."

I knew they would stretch it longer than ten minutes, but as long as they were in the room with the door shut, they would be okay. This is the only way the twins would sleep in the same room-- if they were in the game room. I gave them a neutral spot for the games and toys to cut back on the fighting and one of them telling the other to get out their room. I saw sibling rivalry first hand with Angela and me. We shared a room and got mad at each other often. We would put tape on the floor to divide it up. It never worked. One of us would always need something on the other side. We would get into an argument and would not shut up until our Mom reminded us that neither one of us paid the bills. Technically, it was neither of our room. That would shut us up for a good day or two.

After fixing me a snack of fruit, cheese, crackers, along with a glass of wine, I mentally prepared myself to become Vixen69. I turned on my Hip Hop and R&B station, put on a sheer pink, chemise that only covered my nipples, and slid on a matching pink silky thong. I logged into my page and sat there, taking a sip of wine. When the men started coming in to the room, I asked if they wanted to drink with me. I instantly received compliments for being different. When I wanted the fruit, I held the grapes over my head licking on them first before letting one fall in my mouth.

"In coming private show," I heard the computer say.

I would love to be those grapes. Show me how you would suck on me.

I took a grape, licking all over it before putting it all the way in my mouth. Once it was in my mouth, I played with it sucking it in and out, in and out.

You are so naughty.

Now bend over and show me that black hole of yours.

I have heard worse, and it wasn't like he could touch me. If he wanted to see my ass, who cared, let him

121

look. But, I was going to play with him first. I bent over my chaise so he could get a full view and smacked it, making it wiggle.

`The hole please.`

Hey, whatever floats his boat. I slid my thong off and bent over.

`Zoom in.`

I zoomed in, until it was nothing but my ass on the screen.

`You want me to lick your ass?`

"Sure," I said.

`No. Say Tom I want you to lick my ass.`

"Oooh, Tom will you lick my caramel hole please?"

`Yes that's it. I am licking you baby. I am licking you!`

Guys like him cracked me up. I didn't have to do any work. I had just stay bent over with my ass cheeks spread and they would do as they pleased. Heck for $2.99 a minute, do you really think I cared? All I did was make sure he didn't type anything, which most didn't, because they were too busy stroking themselves. I added a few moans to keep him excited.

"Session ended." I heard that and pulled my thong back up. He just spent almost $30 pretending to lick my ass. A few others snuck a peak. They didn't stay in as long as he did, but that $1.25 was gone the moment they took a look. A lot of men like to be voyeurs because it was cheaper. I cleared another $35 with those cheapskates. I'll take $65 for ten minutes of work any day.

Taking another sip off my drink, I clicked the free chat button. Like clockwork, the men and a few women filtered in. The women normally stayed quiet in the rooms. If they got a show, they only wanted to see you play with yourself. They kept the outlandish comments to themselves. Most of the time, I didn't know they were woman until they told me or I saw them when they purchased me on cam to cam. I found out that one client was a female by going to her profile page. I like sending my clients little messages, thanking them for seeing me and telling them that I couldn't wait to play with them again before I logged off. So, I checked the page and saw it was a female. I was shocked, but sent her a message anyway. She in turn got excited by my email and told me all about the things she wished she could do to my body, and if I would consider seeing her offline. Not a chance in hell, but of course I could not say that. I just explained that I keep a very personal and private life.

She happened to be in the chat room with me at the moment. She sent me a smiley and remained quiet. I saw she had credits, so I knew that as soon as someone else got a private show she would be one of the ones taking a peek.

"In coming private show," the computer said again. It was like music to my ears.

"Hey baby," I said seductively

`Hi show me what you got pretty lady`, NaptownRider said.

The radio station was on my side because a song called *Phone Sex* by Trina, (you know the chick who says she is the baddest bitch) came on. I normal don't particularly care for this style of music, but it fit in nicely with my new career.

Not only did I show him what I was working with but I even brought out my new toy. I pulled out my pink vibrator and flashed it at the camera. I wasn't ready to show him how I worked it inside me, but I did show him how I would suck on his member with it.

I did not know you had that in you! He typed. Then he disconnected the show. I assumed he must have run out of credits.

I glanced at the clock, 12:05 am. I needed to get offline. I had a job to get up for in the morning.

Chapter 16

So, I am sitting in my office doing my usual when I get a text message from Devon.

`Hey, I am downtown let's do lunch.`

`11:30 cool?` I sent back.

`Yes, I will pick you up. Don't worry I am not on my bike.`

He already knew what I was going to say. I don't do bikes and he knows it. The last time I got on a bike was in college and I am not missing it. I had a friend in college who had a bike. He used to pick me up and we would go riding all over town. One night, I had to get ready for an exam, because I was enrolled in the Summer I session. I told him to just call me later. Well, later did not come until the next day. It was his cousin calling from the hospital. My friend had been in a serious accident. He had someone else on the back of his bike. She leaned the opposite way while they were going around a curve. He lost control of the bike. She flew off and was hit by a car coming in the opposite direction and died. He ended up with a broken collarbone, ribs, and pelvis. So, I will stick to riding in automobiles.

I walk out the building and saw Devon leaning up against his brand new black Camero car. His navy blue khaki pants, baby blue shirt, and matching tie looked really good on him. His brown skin, short dread locks, and diamond earring stood out among the wave of people hustling about. It was lunchtime, and they were on a mission. Women in business suits ditched the heels for sneakers and sped past. I almost forgot he actually had a daytime job. He was an accountant by day and a DJ at night. The suit looked really good on him.

"You sure clean up nice," I said, walking over and giving him a hug. I took in a big whiff of his Nautica cologne.

"So do you. This is a new style for you. I like. I see you have been doing a lot of different things lately," he said, mumbling the last part.

"Thanks, so where too?"

"The Old Spaghetti Factory."

"Fine with me," I said, stepping into the door he held open for me.

After we arrived and placed our orders, we started talking. He joked around with me at first about how I used to be so skinny and that now I finally had a grown woman's body. I told him he finally grew into his head, but what he said next threw me off guard.

"So, when were you going to tell me about this part time job?"

"Part time job? What you talking 'bout Willis?" There was no way in heck he knew about the site. I haven't breathed a word of it to anyone.

"Well I ran into an old buddy of mine when I was out riding one day. She rides too. She used to be a dancer, but now she has her own site. I kind of hooked her up with a web design buddy I knew, and well she is doing big things. Anyway, Erika tells me the name of the site, but I didn't think about checking it out until last night. The site has some very pretty women on it, but this one I came across, she looked just like someone I know. I thought I was wrong so I decided to get a private show, and no shit it was you."

I was sitting there looking like the cat that got caught with his hand in the fish bowl. I mean, I did not know what to say. Then realization hit me like a ton of bricks, he was NaptownRider. I had shown him how I give head. I was so embarrassed, the ground needed to hurry up and swallow me.

"Monica? Come on now, look at me. I am your homey. I am not judging you. I was just shocked, is all. I have known you all these years, and well, you are rather, reserved."

"But, you have seen me doing things." I couldn't even repeat what I showed him.

"Yes, and I must say you were very good at it. But, I understand that is business."

"Yes, it is. Well, it was also more of a way for me to come out my shell. I was never allowed to do much with Jamal. I just wanted to express myself."

"You mean all that freaky stuff you do on the site, you never did with him? Is he insane?"

"I just never felt I was allowed to. It was just about him."

"Okay, if you weren't my best friend, I would marry you right now."

"Shut up fool." He had a way of making me feel so much better. I was glad I had someone to share it with.

"Is there anything else I need to know?"

Yep, I have been meeting men online and having sex with them. Nope, I think I will keep that one to myself.

"No," I lied.

"Good, because I don't think I can take much more. This one almost gave me a heart attack. I was scared to tell you that I knew, but it would not have been right."

He paid the tab and dropped me back at the office. I had to admit, he was the true definition of a best friend.

"And who was that?" Anita was on me the second I made it up to our floor.

"Don't you have some work to do Miss Dunn?"

"Oh, no. You are not getting off with trying to pull the boss card. I still have five more minutes for lunch. I am going to spend them up in your face. Spill the info, woman."

I knew she meant it, so I went ahead and told her. "That is Devon girl."

"You mean your best friend, Devon?" She said, looking at me in disbelief.

"That would be him."

"You did not tell me he was fine! From the way you talked about him I thought he was super ugly or gay." Now she was looking at me like I had really been keeping a secret away from her. The woman had the nerve to act like her feelings were hurt.

"Gay?"

"You know a male best friend? Someone you used to spend the night with? He takes you out to eat, and has never tried anything with you. Sounds like a gay man to me, but what I saw outside was all man. I would love to show him a thing or two."

"I bet you would. Believe me he loves women of all nationalities. You could be the green alien female off of *Star Trek* and he wouldn't care."

"So are you going to hook me up or what?"

"Or what? I am not playing matchmaker for either of you. You have to do your own dirt and damage. I will not be the one you blame when stuff goes sour."

"I am not asking to marry the man. I just want to see what he is like in the bedroom."

"Even more reason for me to say no. He is not a one-night stand type of guy." Now, I was not trying to offend her, but she must have forgotten that I knew her little nasty ways. I knew she rarely used protection, because she complained about the way condoms feel all the time. She's also had more than one pregnancy scare.

I ended the conversation by logging back into my computer. She took the hint and went back to her cubicle, doing the same. She did however send me an email and called me hater with a smiley face behind it. Anita cracked me up. She used more slang than I did, even managing to use it correctly. All of the other white people in the office sounded really stupid when they tried. Anita's came out naturally.

I had to agree, Devon was looking mighty fine in his suit. He was no longer my tall, lanky, high jumper friend in college. But enough about him, I had reports to focus on. Well, at least that's what I was trying to tell myself. The revelation of Devon seeing Vixen69 in action on the site kind of had me freaked out. I was unsure if he planned on still using the site, or worse, coming into my room and getting another private show.

I managed to somehow get the reports done ten minutes, before it was time to get off work, not that I would not have stayed longer if needed. I was normally the last to leave out my area any way.

"Monica, do you have a minute?" It was Steve Hanley, the assistant VP.

"Sure," I said. *What the heck now? And, why did you wait until it was time to go?*

"Well, I know I told you that the D.C. conference was the last one, but I need you to do the Atlanta one as well."

"Mr. Hanley, do you realize that when I got to these conferences that I am the only HR manager there. Everyone else is either the assistant VP or higher." *Hint, hint that means you need to be the one going. That is why you have the position.*

"I understand that. The rest of us are swamped, and well, you have been requested," he sounded like he was choking on the words as they came out his mouth.

"Requested?"

"Yes, by the regional CEO. It seems if you have made quite the impression on some people. The conference is in two weeks. I will email you all the details that were sent to me," he finished.

Oh, so you were actually going to do your job and go to this one. Maybe if you would have gone to the last four, you would not have gotten overlooked for this one.

"I will be looking forward to it. Have a nice evening," I said. He said nothing. He only turned and walked away from my office.

Chapter 17

I sat on the plane, staring at my check from *Fantasy Girls* with my mouth wide open. I had grabbed the mail on my way to the airport. Figuring that it was the usual, bills, I just shoved it in my carry-on bag and kept going. When we were comfortably in the air, I decided to look it over. I sat there in shock. I never expected it to be so much. The check was for $4,375.80. I had only been working a little over three weeks and some days I was only able to get online for maybe two hours. I could only imagine what type of checks the full time girls were getting. I made $80,000 working as a Human Resources Manager, which was more than enough to pay my bills and allow me to live comfortably. This money made me feel like I was balling! I mean, I could do whatever I wanted, without feeling guilty about how much I put into my savings account, or the account I have set up for the boys. Matter of fact, I am going on a shopping spree as soon as I get a free moment in Atlanta.

The plane landed. I collected my bags, and decided to rent a nice Lincoln Town car to take me to my hotel. The ride turned out to be much more comfortable than a cab. The driver was very friendly and didn't ask a million questions, or try to scare me with his driving. I sat back, taking in the scenery as it passed by. Atlanta was a beautiful city, more so beautiful to me because minorities seemed to have more of a chance to make it here than in Indianapolis.

My cell phone alerts me that I have a text message from Edward.

What time does your flight land?

I am already here. On way to hotel. I replied.

Mine was delayed. Storms. May not leave until morning.

Ok see you then.

It was very hard for me to figure Edward out. I got the flowers from him once I got back and have not heard from him since then. Did he think we were just going to pick up where we left off from the last trip? Come to think of it, that would be nice. I haven't had much time for my internet hookups, since I became a *Fantasy Girl.* I really haven't wanted to. I get my kicks by toying with the men on the site.

The car comes to a rest and I realize that I am in front of my hotel. Once again, my employers chose a five star hotel. I now understand how the VIP's really blow the company's money. We have to keep charging high premiums to pay for trips like these. The hotel had several escalators, three levels of bars, clubs, and restaurants to choose from.

I get checked in. The attendant packed my Louis Vuiton luggage on a cart and wheeled it to my room, correction suite. Once inside I was amazed to see how large it was. I loved the fact that I could actually close the door to the bedroom and sit in the living room to entertain my company. A desk was set up in the living room behind a bar sized wall, like an actual office. It even had a little kitchen area. I was very impressed.

The rain put a damper on my shopping spree for the evening, so after I got settled in, I went to get a better look at the hotel. They had three restaurants. One was very upscale. Another was more like one more of a sports bar and grill, and the other one was an Italian cuisine. The main bar was like a club, just out in the open. It was really nice.

It had a big screen projector located next to the dance floor. My stomach started growling, so I ended my tour and stopped at the upscale restaurant.

I ordered the roasted duck in strawberry sauce. It came with mixed vegetables that were steamed to perfection, and garlic mashed potatoes.

"Well there be anything else?" The waiter said, setting the plate in front of me.

"No thank you," I said.

I wanted to do the happy dance when I took my first bite. You know, the one that little kids do when they get something they like. Well, the duck was so tender and well flavored that it melted in my mouth. I have had duck several different ways. This was by far the best.

"From the smile on your face, I can see you are enjoying the food," my waiter said. He had come back to the table to refill my glass of mango tea. I had a mouth full of food, so I nodded to him in agreement.

When I was finished, I paid the hefty tab, and went to relax at the bar. The conference started at 8:00 AM. So, I felt it would be best order one drink, but it had to have some kick. I ordered a long island ice tea.

"I will pay for whatever the lady is drinking and Heineken in a glass for me. Hi, my name is Kevin. I saw you when I was coming down the escalator and you look delicious."

I blushed. I wondered if he was here for the conference as well. He looked nice in his business suit.

"You know a pretty woman like yourself shouldn't be sitting here all alone. Someone might get the wrong idea."

"And, what idea would that be?"

The bartender handed us our drinks and Kevin continued to talk. "Well it depends, are you here for business or pleasure, or a little of both?"

His boldness was turning me on. Somehow, he seemed a little familiar to me, but I wasn't quite sure where and when I could have met him. I pushed shy Monica to the side and let Vixen69 start talking. "Depends on if I can please you or not?"

"As long as I can stick my tongue between your thighs while you did it," he responded taking a big gulp of beer.

I stuck my tongue out, licking around the rim of the glass, very seductively, before taking a sip. "That can be arranged," I said.

"So, do I get to know your name?"

"Monica," I replied, taking his extended hand.

"Kevin," a woman said from behind us. I turned around to get a good look at her. We were about the same height and build, she was very pretty, and wore a business suit as well.

"Rebecca, hi. This is umm Monica. We were just conversating over a drink. Would you like one?"

Rebecca did not look like one to be easily fooled. I know she noticed how I was leaning in closely to him as we spoke. I had on a casual outfit myself. I knew that if I leaned in far enough, he would be able to look down my blouse and see the red lace bra that barely covered my nipples.

"No, Kevin, how about we go back to our room." The way she said 'our' was a hint for me, I guess. I would have been upset, but it was something in the way she was looking at me. It wasn't a look of hate, more like she was secretly checking me out. I shook it off. My radar must be out of whack.

"Well, it was nice to meet the both of you. I need to get back to my room as well. I have an early day ahead of me tomorrow," I said. I slid out my chair, switching my hips as I walked away. I wanted to give him a last look of what he could have had.

Back in my room, I quickly undressed and got on the internet. I was turned on by that man and needed a release. Why not have someone pay to watch me at the same time.

"You want to see how wet you have me?" I asked my client.

Yes, he typed back.

I pulled both of my fingers out, showing him my juices running down them.

Suck on them.

I obeyed.

Now turned around, bend over, and play with it.

I turned facing the back of the couch.

"Oh baby I am going to cum," I said to him.

Knock, knock, knock.

Someone is at your door, he typed.

"Ignore it. I want you to cum for me."

I want them to see you cum.

"Too late," I lied. I made oohs and ahhs so he would think I really did.

Session ended.

"Just a minute," I hollered at the door. I grabbed a robe out the bathroom before opening the door.

"Edward?" I was surprised. "I thought your plane was not leaving until the morning."

"I thought so too, but the weather broke. Do you have company or something?"

"No," I said, trying to guide him away from my computer screen. I forgot to minimize the open window. I was not ready to let anyone else in on my secret.

"Oh, I thought I heard voices. Your TV isn't on. Who was it?"

"It was me. I was checking my email and laughing at something I read," I answered, closing my laptop.

"Oh, for a minute I thought it was that guy I saw trying to pick you up at the bar. I was on my way to my room and saw you two from the elevator. As sexy as you looked I knew he was trying to get you back to his room."

"Do I sense some jealousy?"

"Yes, not like how you think, but because I had plans on doing a few things to you tonight."

"Well, as you can see, no one is here."

"And why are you in a bathrobe? I figured you would have freshened up the moment you got off the plane. From what I gathered before, you preferred morning showers so you will be completely awake in the morning."

Dang, I forgot I told him that the last time, "Well if you must know, I was horny so I was pleasing myself."

Can You Keep a Secret?

That must have been the magic words because he started kissing me while untying my robe at the same time. He pushed it off my shoulders and it slid to the floor.

"You're already wet. I can smell your scent. It was driving me crazy from the moment you opened the door," he said. He maneuvered us into the small kitchen area and lifted me up on the counter. I was already naked, no need to struggle with removing my clothing. He put his head between my thighs slurping at my already flowing juices. Missing his touch, my body involuntarily arched up, making his tongue go in deeper. This time was no pretending. I released all over him.

My body still quivering and shaking, he picked me up and bent me over the counter. I was tight, then loosened up, letting his member inside of me. He started moving inside me, slowly at first, then picking up speed. I moved my body back and forth matching his strokes. He grabbed my neck, raising my body off the counter. Now I was upright as he gave me deep thrusts. I felt his heart beating against my back. It got faster, almost as fast as his thrusts. He began grunting against my ear. Then he came.

"Sorry baby. I had every intention on talking with you first. I just couldn't help it. I have been thinking about being inside you for the past few weeks. Then I come to your room and I could smell it calling out to me."

"It's okay," I said, pulling the condom off him. I was careful not to let it spill.

"No it's not. You deserve better from me."

Why was he tripping? That is what he did the last time. It's not like his was my man. It is what it is.

"Well you are here now, let's talk."

"I wish. I haven't even unpacked yet," he said looking at his watch. "I need to get out a suit for tomorrow and get something to eat. I promise you will get more of my time tomorrow."

He gave me one last kiss and went to his room. I stood there, dumbfounded. One minute he is upset because we didn't talk, but then I say we can and he leaves. Whatever, it was rather late. I washed up and got under the covers, falling into a comfortable deep sleep.

Chapter 18

I woke up bright and early. I had to make sure I ate breakfast before my torture began. Sitting through the meetings were like dying a slow and cruel death. The breakfast buffet was very nice. I ate a ham and cheese omelet, wheat toast, fruit and had cranberry mixed with grape juice to wash it down.

"It's nice to see you before the meeting started," Edward said as I was refilling my glass of juice.

"Nice to see you too."

"I saw someone else representing your office and was a bit disappointed, but I made a few calls and had that changed. I made it a point to say you already had the experience and that your input would be invaluable."

"But I barely said two words during the last conference."

"You are wrong. You not only caught my attention, but you caught the other branches when you ate dinner with us. You remember the Michigan VP? Well, he was very impressed with you. Besides, I wanted to see you again."

"Ah, the truth comes out," I said, smiling.

"Yes, but we better get going before we are late. I know we still have ten minutes but it is more important for us to always be early."

Who was he telling? I played this game on a daily basis in my office. Everyone else can be late, but if you are black. You would think it was the end of the world if I walked in right on time. Right on time in my, office for me, translated into unreliable to some other people.

I finished my juice and followed him to the conference room. Thank goodness, this one was not set up around big long oval tables. We had tables, but they allowed for two people per table, facing the front of the room. I took my assigned seat, thankful that Edward's was not next to mine. Then I noticed that all the VP's were seated towards the front, followed by assistant VP's. I was mixed in with the assistants, but in the second to last row. I wondered if they just left me in our original seat or did not want to make me feel like a complete outcast and seat me alone in the back.

The Michigan VP waved at me as he took his seat. A few others gave me a questioning glance before taking theirs. Once again, I was the only minority female. The Atlanta office had several minorities, but they were all male. A 'silver-spoon' lady pulled up a chair next to me. From her demeanor, you could tell she had been born and raised with money. She gave me the once over, before extending her hand.

"I am Georgia, from the Richmond Virginia office, and you are."

"Monica, from the Indianapolis office."

I was glad the meeting started, interrupting us. I did not like the way she looked at me when I said the Indianapolis office. It was as if her office had more prestige. Now, don't get me wrong, I have no issues with people that were born into money and never knew what it was like to have struggled a moment in their life. But, seriously, why the snooty attitude that comes along with it? I mean, must you look down your nose at everyone that did not grow up rich? I looked at her just as hard as she stared at me, until she finally focused on our speaker. I wanted to tell her that having to work for things built character and allowed you to function if and when you no longer had the money. Instead, I turned my head back towards the speaker as well.

I was zoning in and out. I felt like I was Charlie Brown listening to his teacher with the wonk, wonk, wonk, wonks. This man was monotone and he dragged his words. I wondered if he bypassed the communication classes in college, or if any ever told him that he was not good at it. I didn't like speaking in front of people. But when I had to, I practiced so I would be calm and tried to engage my audience. I would rather be in a dentist chair, right about now.

Finally, a break. I took off to the restroom before my bladder exploded. Did this man have to talk nonstop for two hours? He should have known that he lost everyone after about 45 minutes. That was when all of our eyes glazed over. Just my luck, Georgia from Richmond Virginia was standing at the sink, fixing her hair.

"I don't recall any assistant minority VP's at this conference in the past," she said.

"Well, it's time for a change." I was not about to tell her that I was the HR manager.

"Monica," some woman came out the stall saying. She looked familiar, but I could not recall her name.

"It's Ann Gable, from Wisconsin."

"Yes, of course. We had dinner together." She was the quiet one at the table.

"Ann, I am Georgia," the Richmond VP said, trying to interrupt. "I remember you from last year."

"I know who you are. I know who you are and I recall you not saying two words to me either. Now if you excuse us, me and my friend Monica have some catching up to do."

Georgia gave Ann a sharp look and stormed out the restroom.

"I heard her talking to you while I was in the restroom. She is a complete bitch. She had her nose all up in the air towards me last year as well. Her father is the CEO and her brother is the VP. I heard they had money way before her father became the CEO, so if you aren't a millionaire she basically thinks you are unworthy of making any decisions."

"Wow, well at least it wasn't just towards me. I welcome you my fellow outcast," I said. I had to make a joke, otherwise I would have let Georgia get to me. I did still have to sit next to her for the rest of the conference.

"Well it's time to get back to the meeting. We are doing lunch, right?"

"Sure." Why not? She did just come to my rescue.

I went back to my seat and gave Georgia a smile. She ignored me of course, which was okay with me. I pulled out my planner and pretended to take notes on what our next speaker was covering. I ended up writing out a potential business plan for my own temp agency. If I kept working my part time job, I would have more than enough saved up in a few months to start it. I could use two sections of my three-car garage for potential office space in the beginning.

Georgia's eyes started to wonder so I folded that page and started writing out my budget for the month. I always liked to know exactly where my money was going. I guess she was not interested in paying bills, because she focused her attention back on the speaker.

Time flew past while I was working on other things. Our next break was for lunch. Ann was standing by the door, waiting on me. I guess she was making sure I didn't forget about our lunch plans. We had the option of taking a cab somewhere or eating at the hotel. We saw Georgia walking out the hotel entrance and opted to stay at the hotel. Ann chose the sports bar.

I was starving, but knew if I ate too much I would start dozing off around 2:00 PM. Not what I needed, sitting in these boring meetings. I ordered the turkey club and Ann had the chicken Caesar salad.

"So, how long before you make assistant VP?" she asked between taking bites of her sandwich.

"Are you serious? I doubt if I will ever make it that high up." She almost made me choke on my food with that comment.

"Monica, I never paid attention to the reports before but after our last dinner together I started paying attention. You are really good. You're the only one who is not a VP, doing them."

"Well, I have been with the company for almost 10 years and the wheels turn very slowly. Besides, they already have me doing the work for less pay, so why bother with another promotion." I was just being realistic.

"Well have you ever thought about doing anything else?"

"Who hasn't?" There was no way in the world I was going to tell her about my plans.

"True, but if you ever need any support, I am behind you 100%."

Was she for real? This is my second time laying eyes on this lady and she is sitting here saying I have her support. I will assume she is simply making small talk and let it go. The waiter removed our plates, replacing it with our bills. I used it as my opportunity to excuse myself.

"I need to make a phone call before our break ends. I will catch up with you later."

"Okay, I need to check up on my family. My husband is probably loosing his mind right now," she answered.

I walked out the restaurant in search of a quiet area, with good cell reception.

"It's about freaking time you called me. I was about to put a missing person report out on you," Angela said.

"Whatever, it is the first day. I was tired when I got in last night and this is the first real break I have had."

"Well, Miss Taylor, I am sure we can take care of that for you," she said in her business voice. Someone must have walked past her. "Don't whatever me, chic. You may be older, but I will still beat you down. So how are your boring meetings anyway."

"What else, boring. I have to sit next to some rich, snobby lady. She tried to make a smart remark about me being here, but another lady stepped in."

"You should have told her snobby ass a thing or two."

"You know I can't go around cussing these people out. Only you can get away with that. You cuss those crazy people you work with out on a daily basis and they still bring you treats. I did that and tomorrow I wouldn't have a job."

"Well at least you would have spoken your mind. But on second thought, you and your kids cannot come live with me, so keep doing what you do. Go kiss that booty, girl."

"You make me sick," I said, laughing. "How are my babies doing?"

"When are you going to quit calling those grown boys babies? They fine. You are probably going to have a hard time making them catch the bus home. Momma has been picking them up every day."

"The lady that used to tell us that it isn't raining that hard or snowing that bad is actually chauffeuring my boys around? My, my things have really changed."

"I think Momma was so aggravated from dealing with all those women daddy was messing around with that it spilled over to us. Well she is all smiles these days."

"Yeah because he got old and realized she was the only one that would put up with him. Look, I will call you later, my break is almost over." I noticed everyone heading back to the conference room. I was not about to have them staring at me. I followed suit.

Shortly after I took my seat, Georgia walked in, looking like she had been sucking on lemons for lunch. I ignored her by pulling out my notepad starting another list of things to do. Out the corner of my eye, I saw Edward moving to the front of the room. I sat my pen down giving him my undivided attention. I watched as he commanded the rooms' attention. Unbuttoning his cuffs, he pushed up his sleeves, showing his forearms. His muscles flexed as he moved around the room. I began daydreaming about his arms around me. A cold stare brought me back to reality. It was Georgia, eyeballing me.

Edward ended his portion of the meeting by announcing that he was the last speaker for the day. I lingered behind, hoping to catch him alone. Not a chance, Georgia darted up to him like a cat stalking her prey. I watched her laughing at something he said. Looking at me, she flipped her long blond hair over her shoulder while stepping to the side and blocking my view of him.

Not like he is mine. I am not about to fight for anyone's attention. I picked up my black leather satchel and dismissed myself.

Chapter 19

Four hours had passed. I called my kids, Devon, and my mother. I even got online, making some quick cash for two hours. I heard him knocking, but I wasn't answering. I wasn't mad until I went downstairs for dinner, about an hour and a half after the meeting ended. I walked into the Italian restaurant and there sat Edward with Georgia. I lost my appetite. Well, I was still hungry, but I was not giving her the satisfaction of seeing me eat alone. I came back to the room and ordered room service.

Open up. I know you are in there, he sent in a text.

What makes you so sure?

I never saw you leave.

```
So you a stalker now?
No just open up and let me
```
explain.

I gave up being evil and opened the door. All I saw were roses where Edward's head should have been. I smiled, taking them from him, inhaling the fresh scent. He was not about to get off that easy though. He gave the time promised to me to my arch enemy. I stood looking at him, saying nothing.

"Where do I begin?" He said.

"Georgia," I replied flatly.

"Straight to the point, huh. Well she and I used to date a few years back."

"You actually dated someone that stuck up?" Come to think of it, I thought he was too when I first met him.

"I knew her from college and ran back into her a few years back. It lasted two years. It was fine until her family found out I was really black. She never told them my nationality. They just assumed I was white. They found out when I became CEO. Georgia told me she could not be with a black man and stopped calling. I haven't seen or heard from her until this conference. The funny thing is, she saw me check in the yesterday and chose not to speak until today."

"I wonder why," I mumbled. Georgia saw me checking him out and went to stake her claim.

"I mean it was years ago. I no longer love her. It was just different speaking with her again."

"Well, at least I know she is not a racist, just raised by them. She still has class issues."

"I don't even think that is her problem. I think it is competition period. Georgia is used to being the pretty girl in the room."

"So you think I am competition?" I said, letting my guard down.

"Do you look at yourself in the mirror? Baby, you put her looks to shame. Now please come and give me those sexy lips."

They way he was looking at me I couldn't resist. I was ready and willing. He gave me a long, hard, sensual kiss along with a tender hug.

"As much as I would love to be with you tonight, I can't. It's already getting late and I have to handle a few things for tomorrow."

My attitude was instantly back. After everything he just said, I knew he was going to put it on me. I turned my back to him.

"Don't be like this." He came up behind me, kissing my neck.

"Just go before I get more upset. I am not your woman, so I have no right. I understand you have obligations."

"Dinner tomorrow?"

I shrugged my shoulders. I was not making any plans just to be disappointed again. It was time for me to give my attention to someone who has been dying for it.

I pulled out my cell as soon as Edward's footsteps faded away from my hotel door.

"Hey, James, this is Monica. I am out of town and had a free moment. I just wanted to see how you were doing. Call me when you get a chance." I hated leaving messages.

I flopped down on the couch and began flipping through the cable channels. Zane's *Sex Chronicles* was on. I loved her series. It not only turned me on, it gave me ideas to practice on my clients. This episode had women using a sex machine. The machine actually was giving it to them. The fake penis spun around and vibrated. I made a mental note to look up the price on one of those. My body started tingling while the woman was on all fours with the machine working her from behind.

"Hello," I said, answering my cell. I was so focused on the TV that I didn't bother to look at the number.

"This is James. How are you?"

I quickly turned down the volume. I prayed he did not hear all the moaning. "I am good and you?"

"I'm good. Were you busy? You sound distracted."

"No, not at all. I was just watching a rerun on TV. You know, just passing time."

"So where are you?"

"Atlanta, sorry I didn't tell you. It was kind of last minute. I'm at a conference for my job."

"It's okay. You are calling me now. I missed hearing your voice. I was afraid I ran you off."

"No, I was trying to sort out a few things. So does the offer still there for a dinner date?"

"Of course, glad you came around. You will see soon enough that I am a good guy. I hate to cut our conversation short, but I was in the middle of something. Would it be alright if I called you tomorrow?"

"I understand. I did call rather late. How about I give you a call because I don't know when our meeting will end."

"That will work and please have a good evening."

James did seem really nice. Going to dinner should not be a problem. Technically this will be my first real date in years. The last few times I was out don't count, those were booty calls.

My eyelids were getting heavy and I was yawing like crazy. I watched Zane's freaky tales disappear as I flicked the off button. I wondered if Georgia was in Edward's room and what they were doing before I finally dozed off.

I woke up out my sleep, looking for the man I was just putting it on. Where the hell did he go? I felt the moisture between my legs and realized I only had a wet dream. I could not get Edward out of my mind. I lay there another ten minutes willing myself to drift back off to no avail. I slid back on my clothes and went to the bar, only a drink would solve my problem.

Gazing out the glass of the elevator, I see the guy I met the other night. Kevin, I think. He may be just what I need to scratch this itch. I dug into my purse in search of a breath mint. The elevator doors seemed to take forever opening. Once they did, I pranced over to him like I was a super model on the runway.

"Hey," I said sliding up next to him. "You remember me?"

"How could I forget?"

I noticed the bartender was the same one from a few nights ago. I ordered another long island iced tea. He made it strong the last time, and strong is exactly what I needed to do what I was about to do.

"You mind if I join you?"

"Well, I'm about to sit down and order some dinner. You know, a man has needs," he said looking at me as if I were a delicacy

"Oh, and I don't?"

"So, are you telling me you have needs?"

Hmmm, I saw he was ready to play. I wondered were his so called secretary was, but only for a brief second.

"Don't we all?"

"Yes, and right now I have a need, but will settle for something to snack on." He said in slightly lower, huskier voice.

"Really, because I could use a little snack myself," I said with a wink. I was ready to lie up on the bar and let him have his way with me.

"How about we take our drinks to a table and get to know each other better?"

Baby, I could care less about getting to know you. I just want you between these thighs slurping away.

I nodded my head yes anyway. If I had to entertain him for a little while, I would, as long as the end result was him putting out my fire. He helped me down from the bar stool and led me to the corner table. As I sat down, he pulled my seat out and placed his hand on the small of my back. The waitress came over and he ordered another cognac. I had to decline, couldn't risk a hangover in the morning. I excused myself and went to the restroom. Drinking always had this affect on me

The ding from the elevator caught my attention as I rounded the corner from the restroom. Glancing in that direction I saw Edward with Georgia in tow, stepping on the elevator. They were too busy giving each other goo goo eyes to notice me. I paused, before moving forward to make sure the elevator was up far enough that I would not be seen through the glass. I unbuttoned my top two buttons, pushed up my breasts to show my cleavage, and went back to the table.

When I came back, Kevin had a bowl of cherries along with his drink sitting at the table. I know he didn't think I was going to eat those. I was allergic to them. Last time I had a cherry my face was swollen so bad I couldn't even recognize myself in the mirror. I sat at the hospital for almost an hour trying to figure out who I was looking at.

Kevin started right up with some small talk when I made it back. He wasn't fooling me. I saw his eyes roaming across my breasts.

"So, how often do you get to Atlanta? Often enough I hope, so I won't think you are just a fantasy." He said, while putting a cherry in his mouth and tying the stem with his tongue.

I was envisioning him using his tongue like that on me when my cell vibrated. Ecstasy sent me a text message. She wanted to know if I wanted to be in a calendar. Boy she knew how to bring in money. I had kids and an estranged husband. I had to turn her down. Who knew what Jamal would do if he, or one of his friends saw me in a calendar half-naked.

As Kevin watched me, he took the stem from his mouth and placed it on my plate. I was too busy responding back to Ecstasy to notice.

"I'm sorry about that, I had to respond. It was my boss and to answer that previous statement you made, I am most definitely real. But, I can become your fantasy, if you like."

Kevin gave me a strange look. He thought it was rather late for my boss to be calling. He started to say something but was interrupted by his cell phone ringing. He took the call and started heading to the door. He wasn't quite all the way outside before I heard him loud talking with someone. I started to get up and leave. I did not like his tone with who ever was on the receiving end of that call. Instead, I took the opportunity to go relieve my bladder once again.

"I hope I didn't keep you waiting long?" I said in his ear using my most seductive voice. He had returned to the table sitting with his back facing me when I returned.

"Naw, not at all," he answered through tight lips. I pulled my chair up next to him so he could get a better view of the extra button I had undone while in the bathroom.

"You seem a little preoccupied."

"Yeah, it's been a helluva day. Nothing that this drink won't handle," he said, raising his glass and giving a toast to the air before downing the contents.

"Well, you know they say that alcohol dulls the senses."

"Do they now? Well for me, it's the opposite."

"Really, how so?"

"I can show you better than I can tell you, baby," he said, taking me by the hand.

I can't believe I'm about to do this, but I tell him ok and gather my Michael Kors purse up and head out of the hotel with him. As we are walking out, I really take the time to get a look at him. He was one fine man. I loved a man with a close cut. The way my hand felt rubbing across the back of it as he is giving it to me just right turned me on more. The wind shifted and I caught a good whiff of his cologne. It smelled like *Swaga* made by *Old Spice*. It suited him, because he was walking like a man on a mission. He guided me towards a Mercedes, kind of looked like it was the color of a cloudy day. The radio comes on and it is my favorite song by Marvin Gay, *Sexual Healing*--exactly what I need.

He takes a few back streets and pulls up at another hotel. It was nice, but not as pricy as the one I was staying in. I couldn't blame him. He opens my door and starts tonguing me down as I step out. We are going at it like newlyweds. He pins me up on the car and slides his hand down my pants, feeling my wetness.

"I am going to give you what you have been begging for. I knew you wanted me the minute I saw you."

He started kissing me more aggressive than the first time, not giving me a chance to respond. He pulled his hand out my pants and sucked on his fingers. That must have really turned him own because he started leading me to the hotel entrance. He calmed down as we passed the front desk but when we got on the elevator, he was all over me once again. He unbuttoned the rest of my blouse and began rubbing my breasts with one hand. The other hand was back in my pants vigorously fingering my bud. I wanted him to lay me on the floor of the elevator and have his way with me.

I felt the elevator slow down indicating we were coming to a stop, but we kept on. The doors opened while his hand was still in my pants.

"What the hell?" He said pushing me off him.

I turned to see what he was looking at. That same female, Rebecca, the one he claimed was his secretary was on the other side embraced in a kiss with another woman. Rebecca looked up at us with a look of anger, the other female looked embarrassed. I was confused. Was this the plan, to have me be part of some orgy or something?

"I knew you would go back for her," Rebecca said. She had the nerve to be mad when she was just kissing another woman.

"Bitch, I gave you a job!" He said to the other woman.

"Do I look like Cheryl to you?" She spat back. For some reason that name rang a bell to me, but I did not know any Cheryl's.

"Toni, you don't have to listen to him. Did you tell your new friend that you like men too?"

That was way more than I wanted to hear. I know I was not just messing with some gay man. He had been all over me. I pulled my blouse closed, backing away from them. I had no time to end up in jail caught up in some love triangle. Kevin snapped moving closer to them calling them all sorts of names but the one they were born with. As soon as he was free of the elevator doors, I pushed the button making my exit.

He wasn't the one I wanted to be with tonight anyway. I was going back to my hotel, get in my bed, and try my best to focus on the meetings for the next two days. Then, I planned to get the heck up out of Atlanta.

Chapter 20

"I can't believe him!" I was on the phone with Devon.

"He is just doing it to get at you. He is not going to win custody of the boys, especially after he agreed to the terms of the divorce in the first place," Devon said. He was pulled over on the side of the road talking to me. He was glad I called, because if I hadn't, he would be further away from his house and in the storm that he could see brewing in the distance.

"Well this is getting to me. This whole thing is ridiculous. He doesn't even want the boys. If he does get them, he is just going to pawn them off on someone else," I said. I was pacing the floor, back and forth from the living room to the kitchen. A letter from the courts was the first thing I saw when I sorted my mail.

"Look, just think about it. Crackhead mothers keep custody of their kids in this state. You make more than enough to support them. You have never been in trouble with the law, and you are their mother. No judge in his right mind will take them from you."

"You have a point. Women who have seriously neglected their children have maintained custody of their kids. I guess I can calm down. But, I am calling my lawyer first thing in the morning."

"That's my girl! Don't sweat it, but handle your business."

I finally calmed myself down before I had a panic attack. "Well let me get in the kitchen and make Double J some food. You know they will be running in here any minute."

"When am I going to be able to get some of Chef Monica? You used to cook for me all the time in college. Now, you don't love me any more. I see how it is sniff, sniff."

"You are so goofy. You know you are welcome at my table any time."

"I know and I will be there sooner than you think, just not today. You are so lucky. I just felt a raindrop. I gotta go. Love ya!" Devon put is cell in his pocket and sped off back in the direction of his house. He knew better than to ride in the rain. He has seen some good drivers lose control, ending up laying their bikes down. No way was he letting that happen to his baby.

Once in the kitchen, I began pulling out the ingredients to make lemon-baked chicken. Instead of chicken breasts, I chose the wings. The wings cooked so tender, they fell off the bone. I seasoned the meat and stuck it in the oven, setting the timer. This way I could go sit in the tub. I needed to relax. I was fighting the urge to call Jamal and cuss his bipolar tail out. How dare he try to take my babies from me? Who cares that he had to watch the kids for a whole week while I went out of town. I had been watching them from birth. I did everything for them. School plays, sports, the doctor, shopping for clothes, teaching them to ride a bike, you name it I did it. He was too busy saying he would do it tomorrow, which never came.

I sank my tired body down in my garden tub. The milk and honey scent instantly put me at ease. Some candles and dim lighting would be nice, but then I may get so relaxed I would not get out and finish cooking. I lathered my body up until I felt the last bit of tension slip away.

"Ma, what time is dinner?" Jaylen screamed from the other side of my door.

"In about 20 minutes." It never fails. They seem to find the perfect time to disturb me every time. I flipped down the latch releasing the drain on the tub. Reluctantly I dried off, put on some comfortable workout capri's, and went back into the kitchen.

Once they were fed, I tried to go back to my room and relax. I wasn't quite sure what was bothering me more, Jamal acting crazy or being sexually frustrated. Oh yeah, I never did get what Edward had promised me. After he ran into Georgia, he was back to being Mr. Busy. The only quality time I got was watching him in a room full of people. He sent me messages saying that he was going to meet with me later and never did. Instead, I got flowers. He sent so many I thought I was in a green house. He had the nerve to try to pacify me by sitting with me at my gate for a while before my flight took off. I was not buying it. I took off to the restroom, staying until it was time to board. He should have went and sat with Georgia. That's who he was more worried about any way. To top it all off, Georgia made sure I overheard her conversation with someone else about her and Edward's evening together. Come to find out, Georgia was the ex fiancé he spoke of.

My phone rang, snapping me out of my funk. I looked at the number, instantly feeling better.

"Hey you."

"I missed talking to you earlier," James said.

"I saw that you called, but work was hectic and when I got home…Well, I don't even want to go there. How about I just say I missed talking to you to."

"So are we still on for tomorrow?"

"But of course. Just for me putting you off for so long, I will make sure I wear something extra sexy."

"You were very sexy when I met you, but please indulge me."

"I have every intention to do that and then some." I cannot believe those words had just come out my mouth. Vixen69 was taking over. I wanted more with him, not just sex. But dang it, I was sexually deprived. I needed something up in me besides the toys I have been playing with for the past few weeks.

"Please, do tell. So you aren't as quiet as you first led me to believe."

"Led you to believe? You met me at a club. I could have been screaming and you still would have thought I was quiet," I joked. I needed to get his mind back on track and not on the path my dirty little alter ego was trying to take him.

"Well, I guess you are right. But, at least I'm getting to know you better now. I have another incoming call that I have to take. I can't wait for tomorrow. Sleep well darling."

"Thanks for calling, goodnight." Man he sure knew the right things to say to me.

I wish I could say I slept well, but that would be farther from the truth. One moment I would be dreaming I was arguing with Jamal and the next we would be having sex. Not the boring stuff we used to have, but the wild monkey sex I had with Edward. We did it on the counter top, behind the couch, and on the stairs. It was the best make-up sex we ever had. But, right before I thought all would be well, Jamal showed me the court papers of him trying to get custody of the boys.

I woke up at 6:00 the next morning and couldn't go back to sleep. I lay there another hour, willing sleep to overcome me. When that did not work, I got up and began cleaning the house. I scrubbed the floors and walls until my knuckles where almost raw. Silently I cried, removing memories of a failed marriage with each swipe. I cleaned until I had removed the stench of Jamal from deep within my soul. Finally finished, I welcomed the fresh scent of Pine Sol and bleach. The sunlight from the window cast a yellow glow around the room, making everything shine all the more brighter. I felt the weight lift off my shoulders. I was over him, time for a new chapter in my life to begin.

The twins stirred from their slumber around 9:00 AM, awaking to smell of breakfast cooking. I made them country ham, cheese omelets, French toast, and fresh fruit on the side. I laughed to myself as they stumbled in the kitchen, yawning and wiping the crust from their eyes.

"Dang Mom, you are up early." Jayden said.

"Well when I was your age, I used to wake up a little before 6:00 so I could watch the Saturday morning cartoons. We did not have channels dedicated for kids."

"We know Mom. You had a TV with a dial thing instead of a remote," said Jaylen.

"You will appreciate my stories when you are older, and you realize how much things have changes around you," I replied as I fixed their plates.

I moved their plates from the island to the breakfast nook. I wanted to sit and enjoy my meal while soaking up bit of sunshine.

"Is there something wrong, Mom?" Jaylen inquired. "You seem extra happy."

"Yeah, are we in trouble?" Jayden wanted to know.

"No, can't I just be happy?"

"Yes, but you seem different," Jayden said after swallowing a piece of ham. "Can we go play with Little Tony when we are done?"

"Only after you clean your rooms and the play room."

They inhaled the rest of their food and ran off to their rooms. I wondered why they felt the need to run everywhere they went. I gave up on telling the twins not to run in the house years ago. Fussing at them was a waste of breath and energy. They would only slow down for that moment, then go right back to running the next time I saw them.

I gave Angela a ring to see if she wanted to go to the Greenwood Mall with me. I wanted to find something sexy for my date with James tonight. I was hoping to find my little red dress, yes, I said red. Everyone had a little black dress. I wanted something to say "I am on fire". Just as I thought, she was always ready to shop.

"So, you finally gave in and are going to go out with that sexy man from the club. He plays for the Colts, right?"

"No, he is a manager and yeah I am going to see how it goes. He is really nice."

"He has to be. You have been putting the man off for weeks now. I would have given up and moved on."

"I needed to get myself together. You of all people should understand that. What do you think about this one?" I pulled out a red dress from off the rack.

She shook her head no before speaking again. "What you needed to do was get the loser of an ex-husband of yours out your system. I bet if you gave James some it would get Jamal off your brain."

"Jamal is out my system. It is James' first date and mine. I am not ready to go there with him just yet." I pulled out another dress. I realized it wasn't the one and put it right back.

"You are such a goody two shoes. Give that man a piece. He has been trying to get with you all this time. I seriously doubt it if he would run away once he gets it."

I was far from a goody two shoes, but she didn't need to know that.

"I'll see how it goes. Now, this is the one!" The dress I found had a halter-top with a little 'v' slit at the top. The material was elastic around the top to stay in place. It was form fitting around the waist and flared out a little at the bottom. It also had a red belt to match.

"Now that is what I am talking about! Now, you have to get some gold shoes to match the gold clasp of the belt and offset the red. You don't want to overdo it. James will thank you for wearing this. Sexy, but not slutty. You can be a slut underneath the dress."

"I plan on it. Now let's head to Victoria Secret."

I could not make a decision on what I wanted: the thong, boy shorts, lace, or the almost invisible panties. So, I did the only thing I could. I bought them all. Of course, I had to get the matching bras. James said he would be by to get me around six o'clock. That left me with enough time to go home, take a shower, and then get the boys over to Lil' Tony's house for a sleep over.

The woman looking back at me in the mirror was strong, sexy and confident. I was nervous about my date, until I put on the dress. I looked amazing. Angela was right about wearing gold with it. I looked liked someone from an exotic island. My bronze eye shadow and lip gloss sparkled as I moved, checking myself out at different angles.

Hearing the doorbell ring, I grabbed my clutch purse and headed downstairs.

Chapter 21

"You look very nice."

"Thank you, and so do you." I meant it too. James had on a black Sean Jean button down top. The breast pockets were positioned perfectly on top of his bulging muscles. His gray slacks seemed to be tailored to fit.

"I hope you like Ruth Chris." James asked as we sped along the highway in his cobalt blue Ferrari, listening to Kanye West.

"It is one of my favorite places. I love a good steak." I sank back in the leather seats enjoying the ride. With a ride like this, I imagined his house looked like one of those on MTV Cribs. I admired his style.

"So, I guess you do very well as a sports manager."

"I would like to think so. I have made a name for myself," he answered pulling in front of Ruth Chris.

"Man this is nice!" the valet said, opening up the passenger side door.

"Just be careful, this is my baby." James patted his car and handed him the keys.

The restaurant was packed. I could recognize several Pacer and Colts players as we followed the hostess to our seat. The hostess took our drink order and handed us the menu. I took a minute to look over the menu, while James ordered an appetizer--Sizzling Blue Crab Cakes.

"I take it you come here often."

"I do. I thought you said it was one of your favorite places as well."

"It is, but that does not mean I get to come here often. This is only my second time." The first time was for me and Jamal's anniversary two years ago. He complained about the prices the entire time.

"I am going to have to fix that. You are a beautiful woman who deserves to be wined and dined."

I smiled at him and gave the waiter my order.

"I would like the Petit Filet and Lobster Tail." I was going to go with the Lamb, but was not to sure about the mint that was served with it.

"And you sir?"

"The T-bone, medium well." He watched the waiter walk off before addressing me.

"So what do you like to do in your spare time, besides work?"

"Spend time with my boys, read, do a lot of me things. Basically enjoying my new found freedom." The way he was staring at me gave me the impression that he expected me to say more.

"That is not quite what I was looking for. I mean, what do you do when you hang out with your girls?"

"I really only hang around my sister. I do have another friend, more like associate that I talk to at work. I used to have a lot of friends but somehow they seem to have dwindled off when I got married."

"Well, I have just what you need."

"And that is?"

"Trust me, you will enjoy it."

I sat there, waiting for an answer he was unwilling to give. He smiled at me and continued eating his steak. We finished our delicious meal, passing on the dessert.

Once in the car, James still remained mute on his little secret. He jumped back on I70 heading East, then switched to 465N. Getting off on the Pendleton Pike exit, he continued going eastbound. We ended up in the Geist area. I admired some of the million dollar homes as we passed by. With all the twist and turns, it was hard to decipher which direction we were heading, let alone our exact location. The car finally came to a stop in front of a black wrought iron gate. James reached in pushing a code on a keypad, granting us access. We followed the winding path up to a mini mansion. There were numerous luxury sedans and expensive sports cars parked to the left and right of the driveway.

We reached the front of the mansion where a valet stood. He took the car keys, and we were escorted inside. The place was packed. Most of the women looked like super models. They had the long wavy hair, flawless makeup, and toned bodies in revealing clothing. I immediately began to feel out of place. James, on the other hand, looked quite comfortable. Everyone here seemed to know him. He must have felt my apprehension, because he grabbed a Blue Martini off a tray that a waiter was carrying and handed it to me. I downed half of it in one gulp.

"My man James. What's up? I see you brought your new lady friend. Very nice," a Tiger Woods look alike said.

"Dwight, happy birthday. This is Monica. Me and this guy go way back. I have known him since childhood. This is his home."

"You have a lovely home," I managed to say.

"Not as lovely as the lady in front of me. Make yourself at home. Now, if you will excuse me, I have to work the room. I look forward to seeing you later, Monica."

I was shocked. Dwight had no problem showing he liked what he saw. Most men at least tried to hide it.

"Is he always like that?"

"That? Please, that was subtle for him."

"This house is huge. Is he into sports as well?"

"Naw, he was always the brains of our operations. His head was in the books. He is an investor and has made some very good ones."

"I see."

I went back to checking out the house. I had to admit, this was a who's who of parties. Most of the men made big money, or at least looked the part. I spotted a few athletes and entertainers mixed in with the cooperate crowd. The overpaid attorneys and judges stood out like a sore thumb. The people here were not shy either. They were letting their hair down, dancing, telling jokes, drinking and just having fun.

"I'll be right back. I need to go check on a few things and speak to a few people," James whispered to me.

"Okay. I have my drink to keep me company." I moved closer to a corner so I can get a better view of the people mingling.

"Your first time at one of these?" A green eyed, gorgeous brunette asked. She smiled at me, flashing her pearly whites. She had the body of a dancer, and the moves to match. I had seen her putting the moves on a few men on the dance floor.

"Is it that obvious?"

"Relax, you're a very sexy girl. Any man will be more than pleased to be with you. My name is Misty by the way." She stuck out her dainty hand for me to shake.

"Thank you. I'm Monica." I shook her hand and then sipped the last of my drink.

"How about another? Sex On the Beach, maybe?" He green eyes willed me to say yes.

"What the heck? It is a party, right."

"Indeed it is." She handed me the fruity drink and got another for herself.

I checked out her outfit. I liked her style. She had on a form fitting, short black dress. Instead of straps, it had gold chains across the back. I looked down at her shoes, four inch stilettos. I wondered if her feet hurt. If they did, she hid it well.

She stopped me from taking a sip off my drink. "Let's toast."

"To what?"

"How about to new friendships." She leaned in closer to me and whispered like it was a secret.

"I like that. To new friendships." I tipped my glass against hers, making it click. Then we both took a long drink. I was already starting to get a strong buzz.

I saw James heading back in our direction. Someone stopped him before he could make it to us. He gave me an apologetic glance. It was okay, my nerves had calmed down and I was enjoying myself.

"Let's dance." Misty said, grabbing my arm pulling me towards the make shift dance floor. I drank the last bit of alcohol left in my glass and set it on a waiter's tray as we walked past.

A song by the Black Eyed Peas was flowing out the speaker. I had not heard it before, but the beat was catchy. I started letting loose, showing Misty that I too had dance skills. I knew how to work my womanly assets as well. I dropped it like it was hot, even bending over to make my booty bounce. She gave me a playful smack and began dancing behind me. It reminded me of my college days. Me and my girls used to dance like this when we were trying to get the guys attention. Two sexy girls dancing on each other always drew a crowd. The liquor giving me courage. I took her hands, placing them on my waist. I began rolling my hips and booty to the beat of the music, up on her. She didn't shy away, instead she tossed her hips back at me.

James stood off to the side, checking us out. I could tell I was turning him on, which made me dance even harder. I gave Misty another song and then I made my way over to him.

"Baby, I can watch you all night," he said.

"What if I want you to do more than just watch?"

"And what would that be?"

"I can show you better than I can tell you," I said.

Remembering my manners, I started to introduce Misty.

"James, this is Misty. I am not sure if you have met."

Looking behind me, I realized she was no longer there.

"Sorry, babe, maybe next time."

He pulled me closer, taking my lips in his. I was taken back. His lips were so soft. My body melted against his. Our lips unlocked and I stood gazing into his big dark brown eyes.

Overcome with embarrassment from the public display, I backed off him. I checked around the room to make sure no one else had seen us. What I laid my eyes on floored me. People were on the dance floor going at it like wild animals. The women, who barely had any clothes to start with, were now completely nude. One woman was on her knees giving a hand job to one man, giving a blow job to another, and was getting banged from behind at the same time. Some other people were coupled off one minute, then the next, someone would join them. I could not pull my eyes from a lady getting rear entry service, while using a dildo on the woman lying on the ground in front of her. The woman was Misty. She had her legs spread open enjoying every moment of it. She looked over at me and smiled. It was pandemonium, and orgy was going on right in front of me. I didn't know if I should have been offended or intrigued. I had heard of swinger parties, but never in my wildest dreams did I ever expect to end up at one.

James pulled me back into his arms. I could feel the hardness of his manhood against me. He was turned on by the chaos.

"You okay? We can leave if you want."

"We are here now, besides it is kind of turning me on."

I was still looking at everyone one around us. No one cared that I was being a voyeur. In fact, I think they liked it more. James turned my head away from them and began kissing me again. His hands wandered all over my body. My intoxication took over letting my inhibitions fly

184

out one of the open windows. I let him do as he wished. He pushed my thong to the side, got on his knees and began pleasing me right there. I pulled my dress off so I can see what he was doing to me. I prayed no one would come over. I was not ready for that. I saw Misty's eyes get bigger when she glanced over at me again. She was now receiving oral from the woman who had been using the dildo on her.

I pulled James off his knees and put my hands up on the wall. I needed him inside me, now. He entered my wetness aggressively. It hurt for a moment, then I relaxed. I let him take me there, against wall, for everyone to see. My moans began to drown out all the other voices in the background.

Out the corner of my eye, I saw Dwight walking towards us. He started kissing me on my neck and positioning himself in front of me. Once there he took my swollen melons in his mouth. I was in the moment, no longer carrying what anyone else thought.

"Suck on him," James began whispering in my ear. "I won't be mad. Suck his dick. It will turn me on more."

I gave in and started massaging Dwight's penis, getting him harder than he was. When it reached it's full potential I took him in my mouth. James started putting it on me harder and egging me on.

"That's it. Don't be shy girl. Take it all."

The more James was turned on the harder I sucked on Dwight. We were all feeding off each other. Dwight was moaning with his eyes rolled to the back of his head. I knew he was getting ready to explode. I pulled back just as he ejaculated. His sperm flew all over my face and down my neck. Seeing this James pounded me harder and harder. He pulled out and exploded all over my backside.

"I need to clean up. Where is the restroom?"

Dwight pointed down the hall to a door. I staggered in the direction he pointed. I was drunk. The alcohol had taken full affect. I made it to the door and went inside. Grabbing a face towel out the cabinet I turned on the hot water and began cleaning myself off. I heard a soft tap on the door.

"Someone is in here," I shouted.

"It's me, Misty."

I figured she needed to wash off as well. I unlocked the door and let her in.

"You okay?"

"I am fine," I slurred.

I should have been embarrassed or ashamed but I was neither. I was still on a high from actually having sex in public, not to mention all the alcohol I drank.

"Good, I am glad you came."

I handed her a towel. She started rinsing herself off but I felt her eyes on me. I tried focusing on my reflection in the mirror.

"You are very beautiful."

"Thanks." Now, I was getting embarrassed.

"Have you ever been with a woman?"

"No."

"How about fantasized about it?"

"I wouldn't call it fantasizing, but I can't control my dreams."

She moved in closer and began massaging my breasts. She took one in her mouth suckling it. She tried reaching for my sweet spot but I pushed her off. Brushing past her, I made my way back into the hallway. It was empty so I stopped and put back on my clothes. I then made my way back to James.

"Baby what's wrong?"

"Nothing I am just ready to go."

Misty had blown the high I was on. I no longer even felt like I had a buzz. Reality began sinking in.

What must he think of me? Was this whole thing some sort of test?

I remained silent as we drove. The other car and trucks whizzing by on the highway were nothing but a blur. I could feel his eyes on me as he drove.

What was I thinking?

We pulled up in front of my house. He got out, opening my car door and walked me to my front door.

"I enjoyed the evening. I am so glad you are a free spirit. I was worried how you might react. I had to know before I continued seeing you."

"So you want to continue?"

"Of course. What man in his right mind wouldn't." He pulled me in closer giving me a kiss. "How about lunch tomorrow?"

"Okay." I released a sigh a relief. I had not blown my chances.

Chapter 22

My head was killing me. I decided to change up my look a little bit and had gotten micro braids the day before. I went to the African Hair Braiding shop and let them work their magic on me. Seven hours and $180 later, it was finally complete. With me going to the gym four times a week, the new style worked out better for me. Before, I would sweat and my hair would look a hot mess when I was done. Now, no worries, no more frizz. I opened up my Tylenol bottle and popped two pills in the elevator on the way up to my floor, willing the pain to go away.

I saw a few raised eyebrows when I stepped off the elevator and strolled into the office. They were all used to the short hairdo I had been wearing for the past year, not the long flowing weave I had now. Anita gave me thumbs up and whistled at me.

"Sexy Mama."

Laughing, I continued past her cubicle to my office. I saw Brandon, the customer service manager, in my direct path. I turned left at the next opening instead of continuing straight to avoid him. He was on the top of the list of people who worked my last nerve. He was the most racist person I had ever met, a black male that hated black people. He reminded me of the character Dave Chappell played on his show. The black character was blind and hated black people so much that he was a Klan member. They kept a hood on him, so no would know he was black. When the man finally find out he was black, he divorced his wife for marrying a black man. Sounds crazy? Well, that is exactly who I am dealing with.

Brandon made it a point to talk down about the black community, every chance he got. He even spoke negatively about President Obama for having the gall to run for president. He was the first person to not hire you because of the color of your skin. The only time he even opened his mouth to me was to say something degrading about someone. He came to me after he interviewed a woman for the team lead position in his department.

"I wonder how many children she has. The last thing I need is for her to call off because one of her snotty nosed brats needs to go to the doctor, or because of some baby daddy issues."

"What are her qualifications?" I asked, biting my tongue.

"Probably nothing more than temporary agencies, which she probably did not stay at long."

"Did you even look her resume over, or ask her?"

"I looked at the name on top, Tonisha. That was enough for me. With a name like that, you already know she is ghetto."

"A person's name does not define them. It is not as if she had a choice in the matter. So you are saying you did not look over her qualifications at all?"

"What are you? The black people's liberator? I said no! Besides, I had much more qualified interviews for the day. No need to have wasted more time than I did with her."

I went back to my office and pulled the woman's file. She had worked at Safeco, another insurance company, for over 5 years and was the team lead. Before that, she was in college finishing up her BA. Sounds like a winner to me, compared to all of the other applicants I reviewed. I called her and hired her based on her qualifications and not her skin tone. The other three people he interviewed did not have any insurance experience or degree at all. Neither had they been on their last job as long.

When Brandon found out, he stormed in my office, livid that I reversed his decision. I had to remind him that I was the HR manager and made the final decisions. His was just a recommendation. He has been my arch enemy ever sense.

I slid into my office chair, quickly turning on my computer, pretending to be busy. It did not work.

"Monica, new look I see."

I ignored him and kept on pecking away on my keyboard.

"It looks so, ummm, ethnic. Kind of like Whoopi Goldberg."

"Whoopi Goldberg? Are you insane? These braids are so small you can barely tell they are braids. Whoopi Goldberg has dredlocs. Ethnic? As if you would know anything about our culture. Cleopatra wore braids, well at least a braided wig. Not get out my office unless you have something to say about work." I was ticked off. How dare he?

"See, that is why I don't like black women. You are so angry," he said, turning his back to me.

I wanted to shout at him to kiss my angry black ass, instead, I said, "So how is Tonisha working out? It has been a year and I see she hasn't missed a day. As a matter of fact, she is your top adjuster now. I can't wait to see her performance reviews and the raise she will get."

If looks could kill, I would have burnt up faster than a vampire in sunlight. He stormed away, almost running into Anita who was on her way to my office.

"What's his problem?" She asked.

"The usual, angry black woman hurt his feelings."

"Not again. What is his problem with you?"

"Today or in general? If it's today, then it's my ethic micro braids. In general, my skin tone, but that is his problem not mine."

"Well, I must say you look fabulous today girl, what has gotten into you."

"I had a date this weekend."

"Oh my god! With who? How come you didn't tell me? Tell me everything."

"Well his name is James. We went out to eat and to a birthday party for one of his friends." No need to mention that the party turned into a freak fest.

"So, is he fine?"

"Of course. You think I am going to get a divorce and then start dating Shrek?"

"Point taken. So did you let him unlock the padlock on your kitty or what?"

"I refuse to answer that question, under the grounds that I may incriminate myself."

"You did! I know it. Well good for you. I hope it knocked Jamal all the way out of your system."

"Oh please, he was gone before that. I'll talk to you later," I said. I waved her off and then answered my office phone.

"Human Resources, Monica speaking."

"Well you are still alive. I have not heard from you in weeks." Edward said.

"You could have called me if you wanted to talk." He was the one who blew me off for Georgia.

"I tried the very next day, remember. You told me to call Georgia and hung up. I was giving you a chance to cool off."

I had forgotten that conversation. I was no longer mad, but I figured he was spending his free time with her.

"Well, I am cool now."

"I see. So I was wondering, since we no longer have any conferences that maybe you would like to come to New York one weekend."

"I don't know. I've been pretty busy lately. You know with work and my boys."

"Well, my offer is on the table for whenever you can find the time."

"Okay, I will let you know."

"Just for the record, I do miss you."

"Noted. Now, if you will excuse me, I have a ton of work to do. It is the end of the month. I am the HR Manager and not a VP, remember."

"My apologies. Please call me when you get a chance."

Why in the heck was he doing this? He was the one that said he was not ready for any type of relationship. I didn't expect for it to end the way it did, but it was going to end. Beside James has asked me to be his and I said yes. No more internet hookups for me. Of course being with him does not mean I won't be working my part-time gig. As a matter of fact, I need to ask Anita if she wanted to attend Club Secrets' grand opening with me. I received Ecstasy's invitation in the mail and it said bring a guest. James said he would be out of town that weekend, and Devon already had an invitation. Angela, well I wasn't too sure if I wanted her at this type of club with me. Not sure how she would react to the whole private room thing.

I got back to work. I needed to get these statistics together before our 1:00 meeting. I hated the end of the month meetings. Our VP would complain that some of the hourly employees were overpaid. Then, he would go right into talking about having a business retreat. Of course, the retreat would be held in an exotic five star resort. Everyone going would fly business class with all expensed paid by the company.

The harder I tried to focus on work, the more thoughts of James popped into my mind. I was sure he was going to have nothing to do with me after the show I put on at his friends so-called birthday party. If anything, that has brought us closer. I feel like I can talk to him about almost anything. He came by the next day for our lunch date and ended up taking me and the twins to the Indiana State Fair. He was just as big of a kid as they were. The must have rode every ride there and had a competition to see who could win me the biggest stuffed animal. None of them did. I ended up winning myself a Pooh Bear.

"You have lunch plans?" Anita asked, poking her head in the door.

"Not at all. Let me know when you are ready."

"I'm ready."

"Crap, it's lunch time already? Where did the time go? Give me a second. I am finally finished with the monthly report and sending it now."

"James must have really showed you a good time. You never take this long to do the reports."

"This is exactly why I don't tell you anything."

"Geez, I will stay quiet. Mum's the word." She moved her fingers across her mouth, pretending she was zipping them closed.

The humidity started depriving us of air the moment we came out the revolving doors. Today was another 95 degree day. It was so hot, I could have sworn the devil was sticking his pitch fork in my back, checking to see if I was done. This had been one crazy summer for weather. June had record highs, July felt like spring, and now August was tipping the heat index once again. We walked a few blocks over to Champs Bar and Grill, finding relief in the air conditioning.

"I have a VIP invitation to the new club opening up, Club Secrets. You want to come with me?"

"You talking about the club that people were protesting because an ex dancer or porn star was trying to open it? I thought they city stopped the progression."

"Well, apparently not. I just got this invite the other day."

"Well, heck yeah I want to go. The lady has style. Did you see the outfit she had on when they showed her on the news?"

"Yeah she looked good."

"How did you get an invitation?"

"Look, do you want to go or not? Must you know everything?"

"Yes to both, but I will back off. I have to figure out what I am going to wear."

"The party is two weeks away."

I finished up my food, hoping that asking Anita to come with me was the right thing to do. On the way back to the office, she asked me when I going to finally start my own company and get away from People's Insurance. I had to remind myself that I let my idea slip a few years back, right before I got the management position. I had scribbled my idea down on a note pad during one of our numerous boring meetings, when we were done, I tossed it in my trash can. Being that it was my trash can, I didn't think to crumple it up. Anita came over and the outline caught her eye. After trying to get information out of me for a week, and me not giving her anything, she finally let it go. For some reason, she chose to bring it back up today.

"Come on Monica, give me something to be proud of."

"Well I am sorry to disappoint you. One day, girl, one day. Now, can I please get back to work? I have some things I plan on doing this evening and would like to leave on time."

Anita started to protest, then changed her mind and walked back to her cubicle. I logged back in my computer and got back to work. I was in a zone and not about to be sidetracked. I even ignored all the jokes that had been forwarded to my email.

"Monica, I am going to need you to stay late. I have a conference call and need your input."

My input? More like me feeding you the answers.

" Sure thing, Mr. Hanley."

Well, there goes my evening with the boys. I was going to take them to see a new kiddie movie that came out. Guess I will just make it up to them on the weekend. Something told me to log off my computer and to keep going when I went to the restroom.

"It starts at 6 PM. Meet me in my office ten minutes prior."

It has been the same routine with us for years now. He was my floor manager and he had me doing all of his work, while he left early to play golf. Then, the next day, I would have to sit in the meeting and feed him the information, because he neglected to even read over what the meeting was about. I wasn't the least bit surprised when he got the VP position, but I was shocked when he thanked everyone else on the team but me.

I slow dragged myself to Mr. Hanley's office. I was not in the mood to listen to him talk while I hand him the correct reports, or write the answer down on a sticky note while he regurgitated the information.

"I wasn't expecting you until exactly 6 PM," I heard Mr. Hanley saying as I walked in the door. He was fumbling around through a stack of files on his desk.

"Well time is money. It is only ten minute early," came the reply.

I knew that voice anywhere. It was Edward. I started to stay in the doorway and watch Steve squirm. Instead, I walked over to him, handing him the results along with the report I had compiled from all of the conferences I had been to, the ones Steve should have been at.

"Mr. Valentine, I have the report in front of me. I am ready."

"Tell me something, Steve. Who was the person that compiled those reports?"

Edward almost made me laugh in Mr. Hanley's face. Mr. Hanley hated to be called by his first name. The day he got the job and I congratulated him, he had the nerve to correct me and say it's Mr. Hanley. I was shocked, two seconds prior he was Steve. I knew he was only rubbing his status in my face.

Well how does it feel now?

"Ummm, I have to check." He pretended to sort through the file, like I didn't just personally hand it to him. "Monica Taylor."

"Ms. Taylor? That is the same representative you sent to all the conferences correct?"

"Yes, but she is very efficient."

"Oh, I have no doubt in that. As a matter of fact, maybe I should be speaking with her."

"That is not necessary. Besides, she is gone for the day."

I am? When did I leave?

"Well in that case I would like to set up a conference call with her leading for another time. It will be very hard to cover the materials being that you do not have first hand knowledge. Call me back when she is available."

I could hear the dial tone. I guess he told him. I did not wait to be excused. I gathered my stuff and was out faster than a thief in the night.

Chapter 23

"So are you going to call the man back, or not?"

"Not. He dropped me lot a hot potato when he saw her."

"Well you said they were in a relationship for a while, engaged even."

"And what about James?"

"What about him? He is too flashy for me. I mean he hangs out with all the players, so you know he has the groupies too. Not to mention you just got divorced, nothing wrong with you playing the field."

I was starting to regret telling Angela anything, but Edward was being very persistent. He has called me for the past three days. She had just caught me looking at my caller ID, and questioned me once I set my phone back down.

Thinking it was Jamal, she wanted to call him back and cuss him out. Jamal had not seen, nor called his kids in weeks. It only peaked her interests more when I said it was not him.

"Well?"

"Well what?"

"Call the man before I hold you down and call him myself."

I wasn't about to call her bluff. It would not have been the first time she has pinned me down and made me do something. I recalled all those times in high school when she begged me to cover for her when she claimed she was spending the night at her friend's house. Our mom used to say she could only stay if I did. When I protested, she would sit on me until I gave in. And, I was supposed to be the big sister.

"I will call him tonight. I promise. Quit looking at me like you are in the Mafia or something."

"I am going to call you and check. Don't make me drive back over here."

"I said I was. Now help me take this food into the dining room. I know the twins are driving Devon crazy."

Angela dropped the subject and helped me set the table. I was glad I invited them over. I promised Devon I would cook and decided to make an evening of it. I walked into the family room to tell them it was time to eat and thought I was watching WWE. Devon was play fighting with the boys. He had Jayden pinned down on the floor, while Jaylen was on the sideline, trying to stretch out his hand to tap in.

"The Enforcer has one of the Blaster Boyz pinned down. He is trying to get the three count..."

"Do you guys want to eat, or should I let you continue?" I asked, interrupting Devon acting as the Enforcer and the commentator.

"If it tastes as good as it smells, then let's eat!"

"Aww man," the twins complained.

"Go wash your hands and then come to the table."

I went back to the kitchen and pulled out the croissant rolls. By the time I put them in a basket and brought them to the table, everyone was seated.

"It looks delicious. I am so glad I came over. To think, I almost went to the movies with someone I am really not interested in."

"That bus driver still hounding you, Devon?" Angela asked sarcastically.

"Come on now. That was years ago. Can you give a brotha a break? I was being nice."

"Can we please pray?" I had to cut them off. Angela could go on for hours about Devon and a blind date he went on three years earlier. The woman showed up to the movies looking like Rasputia, from Eddie Murphy's movie, *Norbit.* He did not have the heart to just leave her there, so he stayed for the movie. He said she was trying to lick and kiss on him the whole hour and thirty minutes. After the movie, Devon told Rasputia that he would call but didn't. Two days later, she caught him going into work. She saw him and whipped the Indy Bus around and almost drove up the curb trying to get his attention. If a police car wasn't there, I bet she would have drove up in the building.

"...for our family and friends, Amen."

I had my nerve. Thinking about Rasputia, I missed the beginning of Devon's prayer. I held my eyes closed and sent up a condensed version for myself. When I opened them back up everyone was giving me the death stare. You know the look that you give when your mama or whomever invites the Pastor of the church over and he does grace. He starts going on praying for everyone in the congregation... Well, it was that look.

"Sorry, let's eat."

I was forgiven as they started filling up their plates with food. For a while, all that could be heard was the clacking and clanking of silverware against plates. Someone occasionally asked for something to be passed to them. I took a bite of my hen and knew why they were so quiet. It was marinated so well that it melted in my mouth with each bite I took. My garlic roasted potatoes were well buttered and flavored to perfection.

The boys finally broke the silence by asking if they could go play video games once they were finished. I told them yes and relaxed in my chair. I was stuffed. From the looks of Angela and Devon, they were too.

"So, I guess it would be a no for a slice of my strawberry-kiwi cheese cake?" I asked.

"You made desert too? I am barely keeping my pants buttoned now." Devon answered, patting his stomach for emphases.

Angela shook her head no when I looked in her direction.

"Auntie Mo, I want some," my niece said, sliding her plate towards me.

As skinny as she was, I was surprised by her eating what was on her plate, let alone a piece of cheesecake. She had been a preemie baby and was still small for her age of seven. But, she did not let that stop her. She had picked up something and knocked my boys upside the head on more than one occasion when they teased her.

"Sure baby."

I headed to the kitchen to fix her a piece. Devon came up behind me, startling me.

"From the outside, you look like you are really doing okay, but I have to ask anyway. You doing okay?"

"Yeah, I am at peace. I am enjoying doing me and not walking on egg shells in my own house."

"So, what's up with this new man? He treating you okay?"

"It's still new, but yes. He is a very busy person, so we are taking our time."

"Does he know about, you know?"

"What?"

"Your wild side."

"No, and I don't plan on telling him anytime soon. You haven't been back on there have you?" The thought was making me uncomfortable.

"Hell no, that's not my thing. I need a woman next to me, not on the computer screen. Besides, I was scared I would run across a picture of you or something. Not something I really want to see on someone I view as a sister."

"Good." I breathed a sigh of relief.

"So when do I get to meet him?"

"Meet him? Not a chance until I know we are going places."

"You are not right. I finally get the chance to give someone a hard time, and you are going to deny me? How many women have you scared away from me?"

"Whatever, they weren't about anything."

"You are right, but still."

Angela walked in the kitchen, interrupting us.

"You going to give my baby the cake or what? As long as you been in here I want a piece now too. I will take it to go, though. You know I do have a hot date tonight."

"A date? With who?" Devon asked.

"Denise, I promised I will take her to the movies," she laughed. "It's starting in 20 minutes so we are about to head out. The meal was wonderful."

"You're welcome."

I handed her some cheesecake in a Tupperware dish and walked them to the door. Devon and I hung out for another hour before he took off. I guess it was now or never. I picked up the phone and called Edward.

"I was wondering when you were going to call me?"

"Oh, I figured you heard my voice enough on the conference calls."

"That's nice, but that is business. I was serious about it being easier to talk with you about the information. Your VP has no clue. Enough about work. How's my girl?"

"I'm your girl now. What about your ex?"

"What about her? I just needed closure. I apologize for how it looked to you. It was never my intent to hurt you."

"Remember, we were not in a relationship. You don't owe me anything."

"But I do. I realize that I miss you and enjoy your company. I am ready to start one."

"Please don't. I am seeing someone."

"Seeing someone? Is it serious? When did this happen?"

"It's new. I really don't want to get into it."

"Well, I am sure I can be more for you than what he is."

"It's not a competition. Besides you live in another state, and we work for the same company."

"Isn't there anything I can do?"

"Just be a friend?"

"A friend? Are you serious? The things we have done together, you think I can be just a friend?"

"Edward, please."

"This was not the conversation I imagined having. I have to go. I can't deal with this right now."

He was gone before I had a chance to respond. I was confused. He told me from the start he didn't want anything from me. He didn't want a relationship. Now, that I have someone, he wanted to change his mind. And they say women are confusing.

Chapter 24

Ecstasy sure knew how to throw a party. I felt like I was waiting for a celebrity to arrive. Instead of a red carpet out front, there was a pink, black, and red one. Security was out front with the ropes holding the crowd back until a Hummer limo pulled up. Anita and I were already told that we could go right ahead in because we had VIP passes, but I wanted to see who was in the limo just like everyone else. When the doors opened, out stepped three woman, all dressed to kill. A few seconds later, Ecstasy came out behind them causing, the crowd to go wild.

I thought I was going to go blind from all the people taking pictures. I guess after almost getting her club shut down before it even opened did Ecstasy a favor, because several reporters were video taping the event as well. A few tried shoving their microphones up in her face for an interview, but all they got from Ecstasy was a smile before she disappeared in the building.

"Hey ladies, if you are going in, you better go in now. I can't keep this crowd waiting," one of the security guards said to me after Ecstasy and her entourage cleared the doorway.

He didn't have to tell me twice. I hopped on the carpet and strutted down it like I was in a fashion show. What was behind the door was amazing. The club was unlike any other I had seen. The pink, red, and black theme was everywhere, from the barstools to the tiles on the dance floor. There were red leather benches along the walls, with square tables in front of them.

"Looks like the VIP area is upstairs. This place is nice. She sure put a lot of money into it," I said to Anita.

"The woman has taste. She even hired professional dancers."

"Check out the ones coming from the back. Those must be the girls for the private rooms."

"I wonder what really goes on back there."

"Me too, but right now, I want to find out what that delicious smell is coming down these stairs."

We flashed security our passes and were led to our table. We were greeted with Champaign and a full course meal. We had a choice between steak, chicken, or lobster. Now I felt like the celebrity. We ordered our food and began mingling with the rest of the people in VIP. Anita was on the prowl. She smelled money and went straight for the NFL players. I lingered back, ordering another drink. Champaign was nice, but it didn't do much for me.

I sat in the VIP booth looking down on the dance floor. The only thing separating me from the ground below was a thick glass. It reminded me of the club in the movie Bad Boys. The one in which the bad guy was upstairs and looked down seeing Will Smith and Martin Lawrence. The dance floor was filled with people getting their groove on. I took another sip of my drink and thought my eyes were playing tricks on me. James was at the mini bar ordering a drink.

So much for being out of town.

"I will be right back. I think I see someone I know." I doubt if she heard me. She was sitting on the lap of a player, but flirting with the whole table, making the paid entertainers work even harder for attention.

Exiting the area, I made my way down the stairs, making a bee line straight towards him. I was intercepted by Misty.

"Monica, hey you are looking good girl."

"Thanks. How have you been?" I would play it cool as long as she kept her hands to herself.

"Great. How long have you been here? I have been around the whole place and did not see you."

"Well it is huge, but I have been upstairs in the VIP area. What are you doing here?"

"Look around, this 'is' the place to be. I was not missing this for the world. Were you on your way to get another drink?"

"Actually, I came down to speak to my male friend. You know the one I was with at the party?"

"Sure, he was cute. James, right?"

"Yes."

"Well, I don't want to keep you. Enjoy I am going to make my way to the dance floor."

I watched her walk off, making sure she was gone before I turned around to see James smiling at me.

"There you are. I came back early to surprise you"

"You could have called."

"That would have taken away the whole element of surprise. I was just hoping to run into you."

"Oh really?"

"Yes, really. Now come give your man some love."

I fell into James' muscular arms, giving him a tender hug and kiss.

"This place is really nice. Have you had a chance to look around?"

"Of course, I love her style. The VIP area is up stairs. We were served a full meal when we got here. The food was delicious."

"Well I want to see what the private rooms are about. Are you game?"

"Sure why not." I was dying to see what skills these girls had up close and personal. I could add a few more things to my shows.

We moved over to a corner so we could check out the room a little better. All the entertainers were beautiful but none really stood out over the other. It was easy to spot them as they worked the room in their scantly clad clothing. It wasn't sleazy, as in butt cheeks hanging out, but a lot less than I would have ever worn in public. We watched in amusement as the girls would come out from the private area and go right back to work on their next victim.

Out from behind the thick black curtain, leading to the private rooms, came a bronze toned beauty. Her skin looked as if the sun had kissed it. Her hair was dark brown with golden highlights and hung well below her shoulders.

The peach colored strapless dress she wore ran out of material just below her derriere and hugged her curves tighter than a baby clinging to its mother.

She noticed us looking in her direction. She turned and smiled, she knew she had our full attention. She walked her perfectly toned legs over to us.

"I'm Honey," she said.

The name suited her well. I caught a hint of an island accent as she spoke. Her hazel eyes staring intently at us made me envious. This woman looked like she just stepped of the page of a magazine, no airbrushing needed.

"I'm James and this is Monica. We would love to see what Honey has to offer."

"How long would you like to have me?"

"Three songs should be enough, for now."

"Follow me darlings."

She grabbed my hand with James in tow. She guided us to the private rooms. We were stopped by security before we had a chance to pass through the black curtain.

"How much time?" asked security. He could have easily been a linebacker in his college days. His shirt was so tight I thought he was in the process of changing into the Hulk.

"Three songs," Honey said.

"That's $120 up front. You can tip more in the room."

James handed him a credit card without thinking about it. I wondered how much of the money Honey would get as I watched the security guard mess with the computer. Using a touch screen monitor, he punched in a few things with is large hands, and we were granted access. I read the back of his shirt as we passed. It read, "The Secret Keeper". It went well with what the female waitresses had on theirs, "Can You Keep a Secret?"

We followed Honey down the red lit hallway. Moans and laughter escaped from underneath the curtains of some of the rooms as we passed. We came to a stop in front of a satin pink curtain with a black letter five above it. Honey pulled the curtain aside for us to pass through ahead of her.

The room was about the size of a nursery or den. The walls were black with pink, red, and white designs on them. Two very provocative paintings were on the wall behind the red love seat. A pink rug was positioned in front of the couch. On the back wall, sat a leather square mini bench. This room was designed for one purpose, and that was to set the mood.

"Have a seat and get as comfortable as you like. I will be right with you."

We sat down on the love seat as she stepped behind an oriental divider. James took the opportunity to start kissing on me.

"No fair. You started without me," Honey pouted.

We ended our kiss. Honey was standing in front of us in her new outfit. She wore a red, shear, chemise and matching lace thong. I got up, moving towards the leather bench. I wanted to get a full view of her show.

"I don't believe in people watching. Get back on the couch."

Who the heck is she talking to? She is lucky I want to see her moves otherwise, I would have to tell her where to go.

I played nice and sat back next to James on the couch. Honey pushed open both of our legs and straddled them. She leaned in our bodies, rubbing her breasts across our chest. With her left hand, she ran her fingers along the side of James's neck. With the right, she played with my hair. I could feel her leg rubbing against my crotch. It was hard for me to tell if it was on purpose or not. She flipped over and began giving James a personal lap dance, but kept her eyes focused on me. Then, she moved to me and did the same. James sat there with a big grin on his face.

I tensed up when she rubbed my breasts the same as she had did James. I tried to relax, because I knew it was just part of the show and wasn't really trying to have sex with me. Doing another flip, she placed her hands down on the ground with her ass facing us. Her legs were locked around each of our body. Honey moved her body back and forth in a pumping motion, giving us a full view of the g-string up her firm ass. She slid over to James, putting her hands on his knees, and began pumping him in the face. She must have known better, because when she came back to me, she straddled me and humped slow and seductively. She even started moaning with it. Getting a rise, James grabbed my face and starting kissing me again.

Honey was not having that. She rose up, pulling me with her. She pushed me back in James's lap and climbed on top of both of us. I was backwards on James but facing her. She pushed my arms behind my head until they touched behind James's neck. She started grinding her body into mine, pushing me down into James. The more she rode me the more I rode James. I could feel his manhood ready to bust through his slacks. My temperature started to rise.

"Don't act like I am not turning you on," Honey whispered into my ear.

By this time, she was completely nude. With my thin clothing, I could feel her body heat on mine. James reached around us, stroking both of our breasts, and licking my neck and ears. Honey slid her body down mine until her face was in between both mine and James's legs. She looked up, giving us a devilish grin before rubbing her face vigorously in his crotch and then mine. She had me squirming all over the place. Finally, the third song came to an end.

"So did you enjoy yourselves?" Honey asked.

"Absolutely!" James answered.

I nodded in agreement, as I straightened up my clothes.

"If you give me a moment, I can walk you back out. I just need get freshened back up."

"No thanks. We know the way."

James took me by the hand and led me out.

"I want you so bad right now."

"I want you too, but my co-worker rode with me."

"Well how about this. I am going to leave and you just meet me at my house once you get rid of her."

"Sounds like a plan to me." We kissed again before going our separate ways.

Chapter 25

"I am so glad you invited me. I had a blast. Met some fine men."

"I had a good time too."

"I still can't believe you went back into those private rooms, at least not without me."

"Whatever, Anita you were too busy getting your Mack on."

"By the way, your man is fine. He looks familiar to me though."

"Well James is a sports agent, and you love the players. You might have run into him in those circles."

"Yeah, you may be right."

Anita kept on chatting away as I drove. I was trying to keep my focus on the rode. The last drink I had was a bit stronger than I thought, and I had a strong buzz. I wasn't drunk but I seriously doubted if I could pass a sobriety test. I was anxious to get over to James's house and finish what was started back at the club.

James lived on the Northwest side, so I was glad to find out Anita lived out West. It meant I wouldn't have to drive all over town, and then back track.

I pulled up in front of Anita's three bedroom condo and like a good friend, I watched her stagger down the sidewalk until she had made it safely inside.

"What the hell are you doing here, Monica?"

Jamal's crazy butt was standing in front of my car, screaming. I have no clue where he came from, but he was definitely bordering on stalking.

"Dropping off a friend, why?" I should have just turned him into a speed bump and pulled off. But, my curiosity was getting the better of me.

"Well, I have been calling you for over an hour."

Jamal walked over to the driver side of my car. His clothes were all wrinkled, his hair not brushed, and his eyes were red. He looked like he had rolled right out the bed, or off of somebody.

"And."

"And, you are not answering the freaking phone. Where are the boys?"

"Are you serious? Like I would really have them with me in the middle of the night."

"My point exactly. A mother needs to be home with their children, not out running the streets."

"And where should the father be?"

"Do not try to put this on me. We are talking about your indiscretions. I know you were at that new club earlier. The one owned by the whore. Is that what you are trying to be now?"

"A whore? Is that what you call finally getting out and doing things, instead of sitting at home wondering where my husband is or who he is doing. Or, is it not having a life other than work and back home? Maybe getting out to the grocery store every once in a while. If this is the case, then yes, I guess I am trying to be a whore."

I switched the gear to drive and pulled off.

That sucka has his nerve.

I rounded the corner so fast you would have thought I was a stunt driver. Making a few more sharp turns, I found the highway and picked up the speed.

Why the heck do I have to be a whore? Because, I went to a freaking club? I am allowed to have a good time, and he is no longer my freaking husband! Hell to the naw! He is following me.

I would notice his truck anywhere, but the traffic was really light during this hour. I bypassed the exit I would have taken to get to James' house, and continued on 465E. There was no way I was bringing this drama to another man's house. I took the next off ramp and headed home.

"Hello?"

"It's me. I am going to just head on home. I drank to much and am not feeling very well."

There was no way in the world I was going to tell him about Jamal. That would run him off for sure. Who the heck would want to deal with this drama. I know I didn't want too.

"I couldn't bribe you with promising to put my tongue to good use?"

"Believe me, it is very tempting, but no. I will call you tomorrow, okay."

"Okay, be safe."

I made it to my housing addition and somehow Jamal had made it to my house before I did. Once again, he was parked in my spot, the one closest to the door. I had a trick for him. I pushed the remote for the garage and pulled in. Once inside I hit the button letting it back down.

"I was not done speaking to you."

Damn sensors. He walked under the door, causing it to go back up.

"Well, I was done with you."

I brushed past him, heading for the door to the house. I felt a pain in my arm that almost brought me to my knees. Jamal had his hand around my arm directly, on my pressure point. Tears were welling up in my eyes.

"Stop, you are hurting me."

"We are not done until I say we are. You should have been thankful to have had a man that was willing to take care of you."

I flipped open my cell punching the number nine…

"What the hell you think you doing? Nobody is going to hurt you."

"You already are."

He let my arm go, his facial expression changing from anger to sorrow.

"Go in the house. I will leave."

He didn't have to tell me twice. I went in slamming the door behind me with the quickness before Mr. Bipolar changed his mind. I stood by the door, listening until I heard his truck back out of my driveway. He may have stopped me from going over to James's house, but he could not stop me from getting online. I had a burning fire that need to be put out.

I stripped off my clothes as I walked up the stairs. By the time I made it to my office, I was down to my black lace push up bra and matching silk thongs. Checking my account first, I saw that I had 56 picture downloads and 33 new fan club members. I loved this job. I didn't even have to be online to make money. The pictures were $1.75 to start. Nude ones were a little more. The fan club members paid a monthly fee of $9.99 and I already had 515, including the 33 that just joined.

I felt like doing something a little different tonight. I pulled out my brand new blue vibrator and clicked on Free Chat. The men would have to pay to even come in the room tonight. I let my music get me further in the mood as I waited for my audience.

Cha ching!

Cha ching!

That was the sound of money coming in the room, which meant show time for me.

"Hello darlings," I purred harder than Eartha Kitt when she played Cat Woman. I didn't bother to look and see what they typed back because tonight it was all about me and what I wanted.

I moved my body slowly and seductively to the beat while unsnapping my bra. I rubbed and massaged my breasts once they were free. Squeezing them together, I flicked my tongue across the nipples. When I knew I had their full attention, I picked up a bottle of baby oil and let it drip down slowly on my chest. The oil made a winding stream down to my navel. I put the oil down and began rubbing it in into my breasts, toying with my nipples until they were rock hard. I glanced at my monitor and noticed that a few men were on cam to cam, showing themselves to me as they stroked away. Turning my back to the camera, I slid my fingers underneath my thong and slid them down my hips, then onto the floor. Taking a little more oil out the bottle, I rubbed it across my firm ass cheeks until they glistened.

Toying with them was wearing on me as well. I yearned for a release. I leaned back on my chaise, spreading my legs as far as they could go. I could sense their eyes getting bigger as they got a full view of my pink sweetness. I teased my bud with my index and middle finger, stopping before I reached my peak. My surprise was lying next to me. I pulled it out and showed it to them.

Suck on it baby.

No put it in you.

I smiled as I rubbed it across my clit. The vibration caused a chill down my spine. I wasn't prepared for the sensation I was feeling. My juices began to spill out onto my firm companion. No extra lubrication was needed. I slid it inside my walls, pulling it in and out slowly, vibrating me to the core. I couldn't hold back any longer. It was coming, fast and hard. I was in pure bliss, letting out moans until I collapsed on the floor.

Chapter 26

Please explain to me why people always felt the
need to call me early in the morning on my day off, like it
was a crime to sleep in. I did not get into my bed until a
little after four in the morning, so the fact that it was
ringing was giving me a serious attitude. I told Angela to
tell mom that I was not going to church. I prayed it was not
her. I fumbled around blindly until I had a grip on the
phone. When I looked at the caller ID, all I saw was a blur,
my eyes were useless without glasses.

"Hello."

"Baby, you still sleep?"

"I was. It's okay though. What's going on?"

"You know it's after 12:00 noon, right?"

"What? Are you serious? I must have really drunk more than I thought. It felt like I had only been sleeping a few hours."

"Well if you want to go back to sleep I will let you, but I really hoped to take you on a picnic and then to the movies."

"Hmmm a picnic sounds nice. I will have to think about the movie though. I am not into the scary ones."

"I will take what I can get. Now get sexy for me and I will be there in an hour."

I rolled out of bed and headed straight down stairs. Now that I was up, my stomach could not wait an hour. I made myself a light brunch: peaches and cream oatmeal. My micro braids were holding on strong. Just a little gel on the edges and they would look perfect once again. I could still smell the stench of smoke on me from the club. I washed up last night after I played on the internet, but it was not enough to cover the smell. I needed a nice hot shower.

James wanted sexy, so I pulled out my sexy blue spaghetti strapped dress. I chose my lace up heels to go with it. I picked them because the heel was wider. I didn't want to look like a fool if we were in the park and my heel sunk down in the grass. I could see myself falling on my face, and twisting my ankle. No thank you. I do not want a YouTube moment.

Exactly an hour later, my doorbell rang. James was true to his word. He stood on the other side with a dozen roses in a glass red vase. My face instantly lit up. James was inching his way closer and closer to my heart.

"Thank you. They are beautiful." I know I was sitting there, smiling harder than the Kool-Aid man, but I did not care.

"Beautiful flowers for a beautiful lady. I want today to be special."

"It already is."

I took the vase and set it on my kitchen counter, then grabbed my purse and we were on our way. James went all out. He had the picnic basket with a blanket, wine, and of course food to eat. The whole set up was straight out of a romance movie. I was the love interest the main character (James) was trying to win over.

The deli sandwiches were so tiny and perfect. I knew he didn't make them. I figured he picked them up at some store. Who cared, it was all so nice. I leaned back in his lap as he fed me grapes, but had to sit up because I almost choked on one. I took a sip of wine to make it go down. I played the whole thing off by showing him my winning smile.

James sat back, caressing my hair while we watched a group of people playing soccer. The smallest player on one team was giving the other side a run for their money. He was moving fast, zigzagging past everyone as he made a dash for the goal. Faking a right kick, but really kicking it to the left, he scored.

"Stop, that tickles," I said, swiping my arm. James was behind me, rubbing his fingers up and down my arm.

"Stop what?"

I looked down at my arm to see a trail of ants. I started flipping out trying to get them off of me. I was swatting at my arm so hard I had ants flying everywhere. James tried help out but I couldn't hold still long enough with out panicking. When it was all said and done, my arms had red welts on it from all the smacking I was doing.

"You okay now?" James asked when we were back in his car.

"I guess. I know they are gone but I can still feel them on me."

"How about I take you home? You can take a shower, and feel a little better before we continue our day."

"Thanks. It would really make me feel a lot better."

While I was in the shower, I secretly wished that he would come join me and lather me up. I would have enjoyed every moment of him taking me from behind as the water splashed across our bodies.

I stepped out, feeling fresh and clean. I went to join James, who was sitting on my living room couch.

"Dang woman, are all your clothes this sexy?"

I had changed into a beige satin jump suit with gold heels.

"Well, this is more evening wear. This way if you wanted to take me out or just relax, I will fit right in." I was glad I picked this up the other day. I was still adding to the new me, and had yet to get rid of all of the Plain Jane outfits. "I am glad you like it."

"I know you really don't want to go to the movies, so how about we go to the Jazz Fest."

"I love jazz. Let's go."

I could hear the music and smell the food before we stepped completely out the car. Everyone walking around was in a good mood. There was nothing like music and food to bring a group of people together. James positioned our travel chairs in a good spot to see the stage, without getting run over by the people walking around.

"So, this is what you have been up too? You lost one man and found another, I see." Andrea said. She had a red plastic cup full of something that I knew wasn't juice.

"Hello Andrea," I said, dryly. "Where's my brother?"

"Getting me some ribs. So are you going to introduce me to your new man or not?"

Some of her alcohol splashed out her cup when she swung her arm in James's direction. I wanted to tell her that she needed to pass on the ribs. The leopard printed stretch pants she had on were screaming to be free. The material was worn thin from being stretched apart. It's not that she was a really big woman. Andrea just need to focus on clothes that fit.

"This is James. James, this is Andrea, my brother's wife."

"It's nice to meet you." He said it politely and stuck out his hand to shake hers.

"Oh so you taking care of her now? You know she spoiled. She used to everyone taking care of her."

"Hey sis!" Jason said. He stood there beaming with a container of ribs in his hand.

"Hey."

"What did I just miss?"

"Your wife being herself. She was basically telling my friend, James, that I am a gold-digger. You know, like I don't have a decent paying job to go to every day."

"Please, you think you are so cute. I bet you probably ran three miles before you even got here. You know she eats like a bird," Andrea added

"Jason, get your wife. The old Monica is gone. I am not going to deal with her today."

"Oh, so what, you big and bad now? Your body guard ain't here. What you going to do?"

"You keep on talking, I am going to snatch that jacked up job you call a weave straight up off your head. Then, I am going to call the zoo, so they can come and lock up their missing overweight Leopard."

Why did it seem like the whole crowd was staring at me? Andrea stood there with her mouth wide open, while James seemed embarrassed. I know what I said was low, but I was sick and tired of her.

"You going to let her say that to me? Jason, I am talking to you."

I stood there, waiting to be told off. I deserved it.

"Andrea, I love you. You are my wife, but you deserved it. Every time you see my sister, you have to be so nasty. She has taking it from you for years. Enough is enough. You drink too much. And, I told you not to wear those stretch pants when you put them on. Now come on, we are going home."

To my surprise, she closed her mouth and followed Jason as he stormed to the exit.

"Are you always so brutal?" James asked.

"No, you don't understand. She had tormented me for years. I work hard for everything I have and for some reason she is dead set on me being taken care of by a man."

"What's wrong with that?"

"What's wrong is that I don't need to have someone take care of me while I sit at home doing nothing. I have hopes and dreams too. Look if that is what you want you can leave me alone right now."

"Calm down. I said nothing about you staying at home. I love your independence. But, I also love to take care of my woman too."

"I'm sorry. That is just a sore subject with me. You know, it's strange because as much as Jamal screamed about me staying home, without my income he would have never been able to start his business. It seemed as if once he achieved his dreams, it was time to shatter mine."

"Dang, that's messed up. But baby, I am not him. Nowhere close to him. Now let's relax and enjoy this good music."

I sat back at let the music sooth my soul. I guess Jamal wasn't completely out my system like I thought. If he was, he would not have even come up. Good thing is, I recognize it and now I can work on it. I looked over at James and smiled as he danced in his chair to the music.

Chapter 27

"So did you enjoy yourself?"

"Yeah, sorry for getting all emotional."

"You been through a lot. You are entitled to it."

"So, how about a night cap?"

"Ohhh so, what do you have in mind?"

"You butt naked, on top of my kitchen counter."

"I like the way you think."

I reached over, stroking his manhood so he would know that I was thinking the same thing. Dealing with Andrea had aggravated me and I needed to relieve some stress. He grew hard but never lost his concentration on the road.

Bzzzzz, bzzzzz, bzzzzz...

My cell phone was vibrating in my pocket. It was Anita.

"Hey lady."

"Hi, ummm are you alone?"

"No, I am with my baby. Why? What's up?"

"Never mind, I will tell you later. Just call me tomorrow, or later on today okay."

She hung up on me before I had a chance to reply. That was strange, but Anita was always into something, so I shrugged it off. She probably wanted to tell me about one of her many encounters. I felt the car switch from smooth pavement to a rougher surface. I looked up from my phone and noticed we were ridding on the cobblestone path leading up to James' house.

Being the gentleman he was, James walked over, opening my car door and escorted me into his house. His home smelled of lavender and warm vanilla. He led me too the living room and then went back into the kitchen. I admired his Jazz paintings as I sank into his white Italian couch.

"Let's toast." He said coming from the kitchen with two glasses of wine.

"To what?"

"New beginnings."

"Okay."

We touched glasses. I took a long drink of the Riesling. As I lowered my glass, I noticed his eyes on me. He was calling out to me without uttering a word. I set my glass down and moved closer, assaulting his lips with my tongue. I licked the bottom one, and then gave it a gentle tug before giving in to a harder, passionate kiss. James grabbed the back of my neck and devoured my mouth with his tongue. His mouth tasted sweet, just like the wine he was drinking.

James set down his glass and picked me up off the couch. I wrapped my legs around his waist as he carried me into the kitchen. He sat me on an ivory marble island and pulled out a blindfold from out one of the drawers.

"I want you to get the full experience," he whispered as he removed my glasses and placed it over my eyes.

"Okay."

Once the blindfold was in place, I felt him tugging at the zipper on the back of my dress. He released the clasp and pulled it down. I felt a cool breeze across my back as he slid it off me. I felt him move away from me for a moment. He came back and rubbed something smooth across my lips.

"Taste it."

I flicked out my tongue, licking it before biting into a fresh strawberry. He pulled it back, not giving me a chance to finish it. I then felt my wine glass on my lips. I took another drink. With my senses heightened, the wine seemed sweeter. He pulled it away and I began feeling warm liquid dripping on my breasts. He put some on his finger and stuck it in my mouth. It was caramel. He began licking it off me; toying with my nipples. I almost jumped out of my skin. My entire body felt a tingling sensation with each lick.

"You like that?"

"Mmmm hmmm."

"Well you are going to love this."

He picked me up and flipped me over. I now lay with my top half open, facing the island and my butt up in the air. My pride and glory was on full display. I felt more warm liquid being rubbed on me, this time on my sweet spot. He rubbed it on me gently until everything was covered. I felt his tongue licking at the caramel. Slowly at first, then he licked as if he couldn't get enough.

"Oooh James! It feels so good!"

I felt like a volcano ready to erupt.

"I am about to cum!"

"Not yet."

He stopped licking me and pulled away. Something hard, yet rubbery brushed against my lips. I tried pulling off the blindfold. He swatted my hands away.

"Suck it."

I hesitated. James bent down closer and whispered it again. This time I obeyed. Flicking my tongue out, I tasted the dildo. It wasn't bad like I thought it would be. I wrapped my mouth around it as he moved it in and out, in and out. He abruptly pulled it away and moved back behind me. I held my breath for what was to come. He eased the toy inside me. My tight walls relaxed, giving into its size. He began pumping it up in me. It felt so good. I moved my hips back against it, taking it in.

"That's it, take it baby. Take it all."

"Yes, oh yes!"

I was on fire. I was ready to cum--needed to cum. James was not letting me. He pulled the toy out, slid me down off the island, and guided me down the hallway. The cold floor beneath my feet turned into soft carpet. I assumed we were in his living room. We stopped walking. He pulled my arms, directing me to the floor. I stuck out my hand and felt a soft blanket beneath me. I lay down flat. He lifted me up to my knees and spread them apart. I jumped from his soft touch as he inserted a finger and began moving it around, sliding in and out my juices.

242

James was putting it on me. My vagina was throbbing from the fingering he was giving me. I wanted him inside me so bad. I knew by now that he was enjoying toying with me, so I remained patient. I tried taking the blindfold off once more. Once again, he stopped me. I heard movement in the corner of the room as he continued playing with my flower. I could feel my juices easing out, ready to spill over.

He stopped fingering me and began licking me. This time it was different. His tongue made loops around my clit as he licked and lapped away. I involuntary tried grabbing his head and pushing him in further, but he used his arms to hold me down. With my bottom up in the air, it wasn't hard for him to do. His tongue dove deeper into my pearl. I thrust back on his face. It felt so good. I didn't want it to end.

"You like that baby?"

"Yes." I replied. But hold on! His voice was to the side of me. I tried sitting up and taking off the blindfold again.

"No, this is just like the party. I love to watch remember."

I started to resist but he held me down by kissing me. My body betrayed me when I felt the soft licks on my vaginal lips again. The licks turned to sucking, a tongue

243

flicking in and out my secret hole. The person was back to tasting me, and it was driving me mad. My legs went limp, falling apart, no longer resisting and inviting them in.

James came back to me, sucking on my swollen breasts, while they continued to devour my inner sweetness. A few moments later I felt James member rub across my lips. I opened my mouth letting him put it in. I began sucking on it as he glided it in and out of my mouth. His member seemed to grow harder.

"Yes, suck her sweet pussy. You like how she is sucking on you?"

She? What the hell? I am not gay!

There was no way I could answer. I was in bliss. The only sounds coming from me were those of unadulterated pleasure. The sucking stopped and I felt a soft mound pressed up against mine. She began rubbing her body against mine, toying with my mind. James moved away from me again as *She* continued assaulting my senses.

"Yes put it in baby," I heard her say.

She began sucking on me harder and moaning at the same time. I knew he was doing her doggie style. She stuck a finger in me as she continued to devour my nectar. Her tiny finger pumped in and out of me as she licked away.

Oh my god! I'm coming! I am really freaking cumming! Outside of pleasing myself, I had never cum this hard, definitely not with Jamal. *She* did not stop, she continued on. Finally she came herself, collapsing face first into my swollen vaginal lips.

Coming to my senses, I arched my body up, causing her to slide off me. I took off the blindfold and gazed down at her. She had blond short bob and was wearing a strap on. She was the one putting it in me and not James.

"What the hell is going on?" I got up and began snatching on my clothes. I could not believe this had happened to me.

"This is my wife. She couldn't not take watching any longer."

"Your wife?"

"Excuse me?"

I started to panic and just wanted to get out of this nightmare. As I moved around the room, I realized the woman look familiar. Her hair was blond but I knew that face. I walked over and snatched the wig up off her. It was Misty, the girl from the party at the mansion.

"I have wanted you for a long time. I normally don't get involved with his flings, because we have an open marriage. But, I couldn't not resist tasting you any longer. I had to know why he kept coming back to you. I found your website and have been watching you for weeks."

"James, what the hell is she talking about? Fling? Is that what we are?"

"It was never supposed to get this far. Yes, it was supposed to be a fling, but then I had feelings for you. I love my wife and would never leave her. I confessed to her and we agreed to both share you. We want you to be with us, in a relationship with us both."

"With you both? This is some freaky Maury shit. I am out of here."

"Don't go," Misty said. "I know we can both please you and make you happy. I love you."

This chick was crazy. I ran to my car, zipping up my jump suit as I went. I was moving so fast the police would have thought I was fleeing a crime scene.

How in the heck did she even know I had a website? I never even told James.

Chapter 28

I sat at my desk deleting the remaining six messages I had from Jamal. He had the nerve to question me about being at *Club Secrets* and why I was not at home on Saturday. Why he thought I should answer these questions at 4 o'clock in the morning on Sunday was beyond me. Sunday should have been my day of rest, instead I spent it replaying the nightmare of events from the day prior.

"Monica, so you are a party girl now? Where are my kids?"

Delete

"I am serious Monica, who the hell has my kids while you are out whoring around?"

Not like he cared about spending time with them before now.

Delete

"If I found out you are with some Mutha..."

Delete

Clear all messages? Press one for
yes, or two for no, the voice on my cell phone
asked. I quickly pressed one. I was not going to waste my
time listening to the rest of those.

I already had one heck of the night. Jamal was the
last person I felt like listening to. James and Misty had my
mind so messed up, I vaguely remembered what I did
yesterday. Now, here I am at work with Brandon heading
my way. He already spotted me, so it was too late to hide.

"Monica, we need you in a meeting right now," he
said a little too friendly for my liking.

"Okay." I slowly got up from my seat and followed
him to the conference room. I knew something was wrong
by the way, everyone was staring at me. I scanned Anita's
area to see if she was at her desk. Nope.

Brandon opened the small conference room's door
and ushered me in. The assistant VP, the VP, and the CEO
were sitting on the other side. I guess Brandon was the
token sent to get me. This could not be good.

"Have a seat, Monica," the CEO said.

Reluctantly, I obeyed. I was nervous but confident
at the same time. My track record was flawless for this

company. I have gone over and beyond all of my duties to include doing most of their work.

"You do know the companies policy on working two jobs, right?"

"Yes."

"So, you know that you are required to bring it to our attention and we have to approve it."

"Yes."

"Well it has come to our attention that you have a second job."

I remained silent. I was not going to answer until I could fully comprehend the gravity of the situation.

"Not only a second job, but one that is distasteful." The CEO's green eyes bore into my skin. The way he said the word 'distasteful' you would have thought someone in the room farted and he just caught a whiff of it.

"We received a pretty serious email this morning, and it included graphic photos of someone that looks very similar to you." He slid a manila folder across the table to me.

I almost laughed when I opened it. I thought I was going to see naked pictures. They were my profile pictures from *Fantasy Girls*, nothing graphic at all. I was in lingerie, nothing more than what you would see in an advertisement.

But still, how the heck did they get them? Attached to the photo was a statement that read,

How well can your employee keep a secret?

"How do you explain these?" The VP asked, finally joining the conversation.

"Pictures I took for my husband." *Well it sounded good to me.*

"That is strange because he is the one we received the email from, saying you work on this site, *Fantasy Girls.*"

I started to lie. But I knew I was already finished. I should have told them that my husband put the pictures on there without my knowledge to get back at me, but I could not give these old bastards the satisfaction of me pleading.

"Well I guess he got them off the site then."

"So you are admitting that the pictures are you."

"Yep and that I do less work on it and make way more. As a matter of fact, I don't have to kiss anyone's ass or do their work."

All four of them sat there, looking at me like I had lost my mind. Actually, I had, for the past decade working for them.

"So are you saying you quit?"

"Not at all." *Nope you are going to have to fire me, bucko. And, give me my severance package.* I wasn't that crazy.

"Well, in light of these circumstances, we cannot keep you on board. We have a reputation to keep."

"Oh, I understand. We can't have that can we?"

"Mr. Winston, I think she is mocking you." Brandon gasped.

"I think she is mocking you. Don't you have anything better to do? Why are you even in here? You are not in charge of me, or have any authority over me?"

"I am here because I was told to be."

"You are in here because of your skin color. So what, the three of you couldn't handle me? You can't handle the woman you sent out to all of your corporate meetings, because you either had no clue what was going on or could care less. The woman that has to sit with you on a conference call and hand you highlighted files or notes. Did you actually think that he could help you out? All he can do is keep kissing your ass."

"Get out, leave the premises now!" The CEO was screaming at me like I was a criminal. Even his bald head had turned red, with sweat beads forming around the crown.

"I sure will, just don't forget my severance package. And please don't try to screw me over, I have more dirt than you know, on all of you. I would gladly help bring about a class action law suit. Remember, I am the HR manager."

I didn't even wait for their answer. I slammed the door and went to my office to get the picture of my boys. No need to give me a box and have security over my shoulder.

"Monica, oh my God. So, it's true. I just heard about it. I can't believe they are firing you," Anita said.

"No worries, I have always had a backup plan. Call me later and I will tell you all about it."

I brushed past her to get to my desk. I snatched up the picture, my thumb drive and stormed out. I had to laugh to myself as I did it. I had yet to forward the final report compiled from the Eastern Offices to the ones on the West Coast. They could try their best to find them on my computer, which it wasn't on. It was on the thumb drive I just dropped in my pocket.

"Hold on!" Anita said. She was running down the hall, trying to catch me. I stepped on the elevator and didn't bother to hold it open. She slid in just in time.

"What are you going to do?"

"Stay black and die."

"Monica, I am serious. What are you going to do?"

"I am too. I am sick of people like them. I have money saved up. I will be okay."

"Well I am rooting for you. I did want to tell you something though. It is not going to be pretty, but I have to say it." She stood there fumbling her hands.

"Spit it out girl. I promise you I can take it."

"James is married. I ummm, well, I went to this ummm party, a sex party, and well she was with him. You wouldn't have known from the party, because they stayed away from each other. But, I heard them whispering when I came out the bathroom. He was asking her if she saw anything she liked and other things, but what caught my attention was when he kissed her and told her to remember she is a married woman. I thought that was very weird. I didn't remember on Friday, because when I saw him I was too drunk. It all came back to me on Saturday."

"Is that all?"

"Is that all? Isn't that enough?"

After the run in, I had with them, no.

"I already know about it. I met her on Saturday. About an hour after I spoke to you."

"And you are okay with that?"

"Hell no, you don't want to even know the half of it. Those crazy suckas and this job can kick rocks. I am not

253

trying to think about it. I have a new mission. I need a clear head, but first a stiff drink."

The elevator opened on the 1st floor. I stepped off, leaving her and People's Insurance behind.

Chapter 29

A week had passed. I was not answering the phone or checking my voice mail. I got up and got the boys ready for school, made them dinner when they got home, and stayed in the bed the rest of the time. I was brave when I walked out the building, but the next day, reality hit me smack dab in the forehead. I was terrified. I had no clue how to start a business.

Ding dong, ding dong.

I was not answering that. It can get ignored, just like my cell that had been ringing non stop. The only reason it was even on now was in case the school called. Thank goodness it stopped. I rolled over and got back comfortable.

"Get up! Get your ass out the bed. Go wash your ass. Get up!" Angela screamed at me. She had used the spare key I had given her to come in.

"Go away."

"We are not going anywhere." That was Devon's voice.

No, she didn't bring backup.

"We have been calling you for days. We are sick of this," Angela said snatching the covers off me. "Go, get in the shower, brush your teeth, and get back out here. If you don't do it, I will drag you in there and wash you up myself."

I gave her the death stare and marched to my bathroom. Please, I wasn't that far gone. I was taking baths. I was just getting back in my pajamas when I was finished. I did look terrible, though. I barely recognized myself in the mirror as I passed by. I turned on the shower, took off my clothes, and stepped in the shower.

"Hurry the heck up!" Angela shouted, and then slammed the door back.

I was not going to take too much more of that. I turned the shower off and stepped out. I was tempted to put on another pair of pajamas. Instead, I slipped on a Baby Phat sweat outfit. I brushed my teeth and gargled before I came out to see them standing in my room like it was after school and they were on the playground waiting to kick my ass.

"I am up. I am clean. Now, what do you want?"

"Oh hell no, don't even get funky with us."

"Angela, baby, calm down. Mo, we are here cause we love you girl. You had us worried. I understand what happened, but dang. We have your back."

"Yeah sis, snap out of it. You not missing out on anything, leaving them folks. They are the ones hurting.

"You guys don't get it. I walked away from my job, my career. What am I supposed to do now?"

"You walked out on a bad situation and into your new life. It's a fresh start. Besides, you hated that place. You always said you did all the work. This is your chance to show them," Devon said.

"What's that in your hand?"

"Your mail," said Angela.

"I know it's my mail, but I am talking about the red flyer sticking out on top."

"Didn't notice it. Here."

I took the mail from her and noticed the red flyer was for a small business seminar starting at two o'clock today. It was only 10 AM now. I had plenty of time. It had to been some sort of omen.

"You guys are right. I am about to take back control of my life, starting now."

"Now, that's my girl. Me and Angela will get out of your face now that our job is done."

I was glad they came by. I needed the wake up call. What the heck was wrong with me? It wasn't just about the job. It was the break up with Jamal and me running around wild too. What did I think was going to happen with me just sleeping around like that? Every time I acted out, I gave my power away. Now, it was the time for me to get it back.

***

Well I have always wanted my own company. Heck, I have been running that one for years. I guess now is my chance. I had $25,000 from Fantasy Girls, $72,000 in my savings, a nice 401K, oh yeah, and my severance package. I was going to be more than okay.

Before the door closed all the way, I had one last thing to say to them. "So when did you guys become a couple?"

Angela smiled at me and gave Devon a quick peck on the lips before leaving me in silence.

The seminar was just what I needed. They had a complete start-up kit, along with a guide. I met some great connections. One of them owned some real estate and offered me a downtown, historic office space at a nice rate. Other small business owners needed experienced office staff, which I was eager and ready to provide. I ran an advertisement on Career Builder and Monster.com and ended up with a response way larger than I anticipated.

The online office testing I provided weeded out a lot of the nonqualified. The interview process got the rest. One of them included Jamal's Taco Bell Chihuahua. I had no clue it was her until I called her into my office for the interview. She had a great resume and scored well on the tests, but the fire engine hair along with the stars and stripes on her extra long fingernails were not for the corporate world. I had to pass on her. There was no way I was putting my company's name behind that. People needed to learn to dress for success and to stop looking a hot mess.

"Miss Taylor," my secretary buzzed in, "you have someone who has been holding for you on line two."

"Put them through please."

"Monica, this is Ann Gable. How are you?"

"Ann, what are you doing calling me?"

"Remember at the last conference I told you to look me up and I would support you. I knew you were too good for People's Insurance and were on to something. Georgia was intimidated by you for some reason other than that man she left a long time ago. I was wondering if we could meet and discuss me becoming a partner. I have been dying to get away from this place for years but never had somewhere I wanted to be."

I almost dropped the phone. Ann had money, deep-rooted money going back to her ancestors. What the heck did she need me for?

"I know you don't know me well, but I have been watching your career for years. You should have been the VP a long time ago. I feel that, together, we can take your new company nationally and help other women make it in the good ole boy system. I have personally witnessed some of your employees first hand. Brandon would have had a heart attack if he knew the new employee he was gloating over had come from the company you own. She was highly trained and ready for the position from day one."

"Wow, I don't know what to say. We can definitely get together, because I can use a great partner. Business is booming way more than I could have ever anticipated. An office in another city is way more than I could have dreamed of. Let's set something for later in the week."

"Great."

"Good, now if you will excuse me I have a lunch meeting."

I disconnected the call and smiled at the handsome man standing in my doorway. I had given in weeks ago and called Edward. He had been by my side from the first day I signed the lease to my office.

"I brought Japanese."

"Hmmm, I had something a little more light in mind," I purred. "Now please come in and shut the door. This is one secret I plan on keeping."

The End

LaVergne, TN USA
05 November 2010
203721LV00009B/100/P

9 780984 350476